THE SNOW FORESTERS

THE SNOW FORESTERS

AND OTHER TALES OF THE

SLIGHTLY EERIE

DAVID PHELPS

ILLUSTRATIONS BY VERONIQUE AVON

Matador
9 Priory Business Park,
Wistow Road, Kibworth Beauchamp,
Leicestershire. LE8 0RX
Tel: 0116 279 2299
Email: books@troubador.co.uk
Web: www.troubador.co.uk/matador
Twitter: @matadorbooks

ISBN 978 1789010 220
British Library Cataloguing in Publication Data.
A catalogue record for this book is available from the British Library.

Printed and Bound in the UK by 4edge Limited
Typeset in Minion Pro 11pt by Troubador Publishing Ltd, Leicester, UK

Matador is an imprint of Troubador Publishing Ltd

My grateful thanks to the following people who gave me encouragement to carry on with this book:

Valerie Dean, James Phelps, Marina Phelps, Barbara Bromhead-Wragg, Kirst Hartsiotis, Sue Allonby, Janet Dowling, Glenn Smith and Wendy Phelps.

My thanks also to Hannah Dakin, Heidi Hurst, Jonathan White and all the other people at Troubador Publishing who made the idea reality.

You can find more about David Phelps at
www.davidphelpswrites.co.uk

And more work by Veronique Avon at
www.atelierveronique.co.uk

CONTENTS

WHY THE STORY YOU TELL IS IMPORTANT

"Fairy tales are more than true, not because they tell us that dragons exist, but because they tell us that dragons can be beaten."

G.K. Chesterton

We know we live in a time when many dragons exist, those of climate change, global inequality and probably quite a few others that you can bring to mind. So what are the stories we are telling ourselves about how they can be beaten?

Folk tales are never neutral but they are not necessarily always wise and beneficent as anyone who has come across the tale of Little St Hugh of Lincoln, used to justify medieval anti-Semitism, will understand. Its malignity is obvious, so much so that it has lost its power and most people would only find it repugnant. But there are more subtle narratives out there. Perhaps you heard them down the pub or read a story in a newspaper. They tell the story of "The Other", the outsider who is not one of us. How dangerous they are, what a threat to our cosy existence. Or perhaps you are listening to stories that are even more dangerous, those that tell us that this is the way the world works, you can't do anything to change it and you would be a fool to try.

If you read the stories in any book of folk tales you will come across quite a lot of fools. Strangely they make friends with all and sundry and have a habit of killing dragons and generally making the world better. Perhaps they were too foolish to understand the other stories they were told; perhaps not.

There is a famous late-eighteenth-century cartoon by James Gillray called French Liberty, British Slavery. In one half of the cartoon a French peasant sits in front of his cold hearth chewing a raw onion and congratulating himself for living in a land of liberty. In the other John Bull tucks into a great slab of roast beef, complaining that he lives in a land of tyranny and high taxes. Both are right and both are wrong. It all depends what story you tell yourself and sometimes you might be telling yourself the wrong story.

Storytelling, in all its many guises, is the way we make sense of the madness around us that we choose to call reality. Listening to or reading folk tales you can become aware that there are a lot of different possibilities out there, that the world is more magical than we might think it, that there are more creative solutions to problems that we fear are impossible. It may have been ever thus but there now seems to be too many people out there who want to limit the stories we listen to. If you liked that you must like this, don't go searching for something different; the world is a scary place, don't go exploring but stick with the stories that tell you that you are right and everyone else is wrong headed. So walls are built and there is always someone who makes a surprisingly good living out of selling the bricks.

Unlike politicians, folk tales do not shout, telling you what to believe. For good or ill they are more subtle than that. You can listen to a folk tale many times, think you know it, when suddenly your heart will open up to a new meaning, because that was what you needed to learn at that moment. And, as a storyteller, I am convinced that no two people hear the same story when I am telling it.

In Robert Irwin's latest book, Wonders Will Never Cease, the protagonist, Earl Rivers, listens to a telling of Jack the Giant Killer and is outraged. To him the peasant Jack is a thief and a murderer, the Giant, an aristocrat like himself, has every right to his goose, his harp, his castle and the rest of his property. We all bring our prejudices to the story though, speaking as a peasant, it does no harm to consider the Giant's point of view for once.

If we only listen to the stories that limit us, the danger is not only that we will limit ourselves but also we will inevitably start telling stories of limitation.

So read and listen to the stories of how the dragons of greed and the giants of despair can be beaten. Then you might be able to tell the stories that you want told.

THE SNOW
FORESTERS

(With thanks to Anthony Nanson, who first made me aware of the existence of such creatures.)

It had been another bad night. He had woken from a dream of dread and failed to get back to sleep. With dawn he had dozed and then slept through the alarm clock.

The self-catering cottage had been a good idea. He could get up when he felt more rested, have a good breakfast, put the gloom of the night behind him and still get in an afternoon's walk in the snow.

He had planned his route the previous evening so now drove directly to the pub where he had intended to have lunch. It went by an intriguing name, "The Snow Forester". He was glad to find it oak panelled, with a roaring log fire and not at all disheartened that he was the only patron and the young barmaid not inclined to pay too much attention to him. He confined himself to half a pint and a steak and ale pie. The beer was reasonable but the pie was salty. He rechecked his route on the map, anticipating the pleasures to come, a walk through woodland in freshly fallen snow.

On a trip to the loo he searched the walls for any notice that explained the strange name but there was nothing. The sign outside only bore the name of the pub and the brewery, no pictorial representation of a snow forester that might have given him a clue. At the end of his meal he took his empty glass back to the bar.

"Unusual name."

"What?"

"The Snow Forester. Do you know where it comes from?"

She looked at him as if it was the most stupid question anyone had ever asked her. "Dunno. Something local I guess."

He was almost out of the door when he noticed a large bowl by the door. It was full of salt.

"What's this?"

She shrugged. "Some superstition. You're supposed to take a pinch of it if you are leaving the pub in the dark, for luck."

"Then I won't need it then."

But she had already moved off into the public bar.

When he got out of the pub he found a thick mist had descended. For a moment he considered changing his plans but walking in mist in snowy woodland had its own charms. He drove about a mile to the lay-by where he could park. The road had been gritted but he had taken alcohol so was careful. Boots and cold weather gear on, map checked again, then off along the path that led into the trees.

His boots crunched on virgin snow, above him the mist swirled around the branches of the trees like wraiths. Close to the path were straight young ash and silver birch but off in the mist he caught glances of gnarled, ancient oaks. He was not a romantic and knew there were very few patches of the old wild wood left, if any, but it was possible to imagine that this could be untouched forest, millennia old. When he stopped, the forest was silent. He waited for a bird call but there was nothing.

Cold stung his face but his body was warm. He carried on at a steady pace. Back in London his colleagues would be looking at their watches and know they still had three hours to work.

Something gigantic loomed out of the mist, something that looked like a huge skull. The mist billowed and cleared a little and he saw that it was only some sort of building, with two upper windows and a central door. That silly human trait that can see faces in anything had given him a momentary jolt. There was a cross on top of the roof. An aficionado of visiting old churches, he tried the door and was surprised when it opened to his push.

Gloom and the musty smell of an unheated building. His hand searched on the wall for a switch. Cold stone but then metal. When he flicked it down a sour yellow light glimmered shakily from a bare, dusty bulb, illuminating a stark interior of dark wooden pews with their backs turned to him. No ornament, so some extreme puritan sect that might still exist in such an out-of-the-way spot. He let the heavy wooden door shut behind him, the echo rattling through the empty building. He was propelled further into the church, looking for some local history, but the plain white walls told him nothing.

He took out his map from the pocket of his anorak, checked the route and found where he must be. Chapel (dis). He did not remember spotting it during the planning. Disused, yet he had found the door unlocked, presumably a not very careful guardian. There was a heavy thump on the roof of the chapel. He ducked, his heart racing but then realised it must be a clump of snow falling from the trees. He smiled, and the scratching on the windows could only be branches. But it made the place feel desolate. He felt that creepy feeling that sometimes came over him in empty churches, of being watched by generations of disapproving churchgoers. Chapel-goers must be even worse. He left, the door banging behind him, and set off at a fast pace along the path.

Soon he was warm again. He concentrated on enjoying the pull of his muscles as he walked but the visit to the chapel had made him feel spooked. He stopped for a moment. Still the forest was completely quiet. He had not seen another human being for, he checked his watch, three-quarters of an hour. Normally he would be happy to have achieved such solitude but he admitted to himself that he would like to come across a fellow human. He might be the only soul in the whole of this forest. He shivered and set off again at a faster pace. He had reckoned that the walk would take him about two hours. He was a quarter through it. But how long had he spent in the chapel? He still had over an hour and a half before he saw his car again. No, enjoy this! He was walking through snow and mist in a safe and beautiful English wood. Atmospheric was the word for it, stupid to wish his life away. He set off at a faster pace.

He was on the ground, his face in snow and a pain in his left knee and his foot was being held. He pulled himself up on his elbows and looked backwards. It was a bramble. He had been a bit careless, nothing more. He smiled as he gingerly lifted himself up and dusted the snow off his anorak. No great harm done. Checking his watch he found five minutes had passed since he had last looked at it. Had he been walking that long? Had he knocked himself out for a brief while? He felt a little light headed but that might be the beer. Although the forest was still, there must have been a breath of wind off to his right because the branches of the larger trees moved like something advancing. He had become chilled by the snow and needed to get moving.

As he walked his hand moved to his map pocket. It was empty. He patted the other pockets in a futile gesture. He always kept his map in that pocket. He had last looked at it in the chapel. He must have left it there. He turned around, wondering if he ought to go back for it but then another gust of wind rattled some branches along the track from which he had come. He turned round again and studied the path in front of him. If he remembered the route it would take him on a loop through the forest and bring him back to the road. A hundred yards of road walking and then he would be back at his car. He thought fondly of his car, the joy he would feel at seeing it, his adventure successfully over. He had left a thermos of coffee on the passenger seat. It would be good to drink that and then drive back to his cottage. A hot bath was what he needed now. All he had to do was make sure he did not take any of the smaller side tracks in the mist and he would be fine.

He walked on, a pain in his knee but he had stood about dithering for too long. A brisk pace should put it right. The snow along the path was thicker now in the centre of the wood. Before long he was trudging through it. He had to admit to himself that, with the cold and the mist, this was no longer pleasant. Something thumped off to his right, stopping him in his tracks, but there was nothing there. Some more snow falling off branches? It came into his mind that he had not told anyone where he was going. Who was there to tell? The other holiday cottages near him were empty. The barmaid would have thought him stupid if he tried to tell her of his route in case anything should happen. What could happen?

Through the thick mist he saw something solid beginning to loom. Oh God, was he going around in circles and had come back to the chapel? But no, this was a different outline, squatter, a cottage. From one window a pale yellow light barely shone out through the fog. He would be alright now. The people would be able to give him directions, even, he thought guiltily, give him a lift back to his car, a break from this terrible solitude. He almost ran through the thick snow towards the house.

He stood like a child, looking in at the tableau beyond the window. A simple room, in the centre a man and a woman sat at a table. A cat was curled up on a chair by the fire. He lifted his hand to knock on the pane when he noticed something odd. The couple were both dressed in costume that dated from a hundred years before. The light came from the globe of a paraffin lamp in the middle of the table. He looked more closely and saw that both had their eyes open and were staring, unblinking, into space. However hard he knocked they would not hear him. The man, the woman, even the cat, were dead, overtaken by some terrible miasma that had crept into their room and taken them unawares. All this had happened a century before and was being shown him as a foretaste of his own death. His spine froze with terror. He turned around and ran from the horror, not caring where he went, just to get away from whatever was toying with him.

He held onto a tree, trying to regain his breath. Now he dared to look back but the mist had already hidden the cottage, if he had even ever seen it. He studied the gnarled bark of the tree, which was real and substantial. He put his cheek against it and the damp smell gave him some comfort. He saw that he was still on a path, either side were tall trees and impenetrable brambles. The path led off into the mist. It was untouched, not even bird or fox prints to show him that he was not alone. But where did it lead? Grudgingly he put his foot forward. He had no choice. He could never turn back in the direction of the cottage. Not finding it would be almost as bad as seeing it again.

Unsteadily he walked into the mist that wrapped around him like a magician's cloak. He thought he heard tinkling laughter from somewhere behind him but he had no wish to stop. He walked on, gaining confidence with each step, each yard that took him away from something that could not have happened. In an hour or so he would be back at his car.

But it was getting dark. He looked at his watch. It was only three o'clock. There should still be a good hour and a half of serviceable light. More than enough time, as long as he was on the right path. It must be the mist, making it unnaturally dark. He stopped walking and looked back. It had been his imagination playing tricks. He shouldn't have had the beer. The forest was silent, gloomy. Far away there was something moving through the forest. It was coming his way. There were supposed to be wild boar in parts of the forest but surely they would keep away from humans? There was also something moving on the other side of the path. It too seemed to be coming his way. He turned and he walked. It was a determined pace but he did not want to run. He could not help but look over his shoulder every so often but saw nothing. He must keep going.

A pain scythed through his abdomen. Stitch, he would have to stop. Out of the corner of his eye he saw a light. He stood up, the pain forgotten. There was another light on the other side of the path, no, there were three moving towards him, like lamplight, barely perceptible in the mist and white rather than the yellow that had been coming from the cottage. Then he could see another, more distant but rapidly catching up. For a moment he thought they might be coming to rescue him, but who knew he was here?

A lethargy rooted him to the spot. They were close now. What was the point in running? The lights came not from lamps, but from within their bodies. They were smaller than him but an almost human shape, although their faces were wizened, old, so old. They came towards him in a gliding motion, as if not really walking. The part of his brain that liked to label things struggled to find anything to explain what was approaching him.

The nearest of the creatures came up to him and touched his upper right arm. Immediately a coldness flowed through him as if his blood had been frozen. The second came forward but it was twittering like an angry blackbird. It shoved the first who let go its grip. Immediately the man felt he was awakening but into the nightmare. It waved at him as if shooing him off. He was being spared. He turned and he ran as fast as his layers of clothing, his heavy boots and the virgin snow would allow him. Behind him he heard some more excited twittering. He turned and saw all four things once again pursuing him. He had not been spared, they just wanted to prolong the hunt.

There was pain in his side and pain in his throat. He was stumbling rather than running. Why was this happening to him? Tears of unfairness stung his eyes. He could not dare a look back, but, over his stumbling, he was sure he could hear their twittering.

Were the trees getting more spaced out? If he could get out of the forest then he had a chance. There was a light, he was sure of it. Could there be somewhere that he could find safety? He tried to run faster. Either side of him he felt space opening up but there was something in front of him from which a light was coming. With horror he saw that it was the same white light that was coming from the creatures. He stopped, there was no more point in running. The mist partly cleared. In front of him was a mound, like a huge anthill. A door seemed to have opened, from which the light was coming. In the light he was sure he could see more of the creatures. He was calm, the uncertainty was over.

He felt both his arms grabbed, again that awful coldness, and he was taken into the snow foresters' mound.

UNWANTED GUESTS

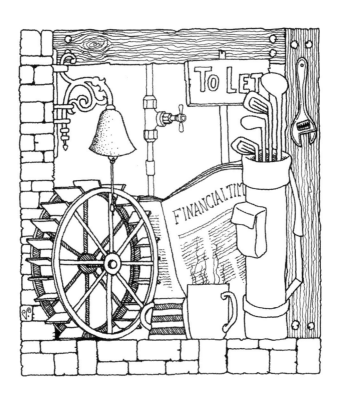

Harry Burbage sat back in his new kitchen and smelled the coffee. Looking out of the window and not having the most original mind, the thought came to him, "Lord of all he surveys."

Strictly speaking, the hills rising up above his house were not his, but the large paddocks were, the newly gutted and refurbished Old Rectory was, likewise the shiny kitchen in which he sat. The house pleased him. When he got tired of it, the place would make excellent holiday cottages.

If the hills were not his, he was the owner of several pockets of the county of Herefordshire. Like a Norman baron his land was spread widely because he had bought up large country houses cheaply, often when the commune that had tried to make a home there had failed, and he turned them into fairy-tale locations in which the people of the West Midlands could have fairy-tale weddings.

Thinking about his net worth always made him smile and he was smiling to himself now, sitting in his warm kitchen drinking recently-brewed coffee. Just one thing wrong, there was something or someone in one of his paddocks. At first he had thought it was a scarecrow, but, although he took no interest in agriculture, he realised there was little point in putting a scarecrow in a horse paddock. The other strange thing was that it seemed every time he blinked or took a sip of coffee the figure moved, coming ever so slightly closer.

He was trying to stare at the thing without blinking,

just to prove himself wrong, when there was a sudden draught and his wife came into the kitchen wearing a fluffy white dressing gown that matched his own.

"This house is bloody freezing." Morwenna was a London girl and found Harry's determination to be a country gentleman incomprehensible. He chose not to respond and concentrated on the figure in the paddock.

She poured herself a mug of coffee and stared angrily at her silent husband. "You haven't had a stroke or something, have you?"

"What!"

"If I speak I normally expect you to answer."

"Sorry. I was watching someone in the paddock."

"Well, good luck to them. They're braver than I am."

"You really ought to give riding another chance. It was just bad luck that one bit you."

Morwenna made a sound of derision surprisingly like a horse. She took a big draught of coffee but still she shivered.

Her husband turned to look at her for the first time that morning. "In this county you meet some very good contacts in the saddle."

"Then you try it." She went over to the window. "So where is this trespasser?"

Harry stood beside her. "Over… oh, he's gone."

"Probably one of the locals wanting a job, or a tramp; probably frightened the lord of the manor would set the dogs on him and changed his mind."

Part of Harry disliked the way Morwenna made fun of him. Technically he was now lord of several manors.

He often wondered if he would ever have the nerve to ring up a restaurant and say, "This is Lord Burbage speaking."

Morwenna shivered again. "I'm going to have a shower. See if that warms me up."

Alone in the kitchen, Harry picked up his financial paper and started checking it to see if there was anything that should be of interest to him. Some upwardly-mobile shares were just what he needed right now.

The doorbell rang. Harry cursed. If that was a tramp wanting a handout then he would get short shrift. Even if it was someone wanting work he would be told in no uncertain terms that one did not go pestering one's betters this early on a Saturday morning.

Harry checked the knot of his dressing gown and pulled the collar up around his neck. He went into the hall and opened the door, rehearsing his anger.

It was the smell that caught him first. It hit the back of his throat and almost made him retch, the smell of bodily corruption. With watery eyes he tried to focus on the brown wizened figure in front of him.

"You'll get no luck here maister. You'd be better leavin."

Harry was speechless. He tried to think of something to say, but then saw that the old man was moving his mouth about in a most disgusting manner, almost as if he was collecting saliva in order to spit. The evil old lips started to purse. Instinctively Harry closed his eyes and brought his hands up to his face.

But no spit came. For several seconds Harry held the

pose then nervously looked though his fingers. There was no one there.

He looked left and right. No sign. For such an old man he seemed to be able to move at some speed. Thoughtfully Harry closed the door. The scream made him jump convulsively.

"Morwenna!" Harry raced up the stairs at a speed that his doctor would not have advised.

Bursting though the bathroom door he was shocked to see his wife cowering at the bottom of the shower cubicle, the curtain wrapped around her. Before he could say anything she held out her arms to him in a pleading way. He knelt down beside her.

"What on earth happened?"

She could barely speak through her sobs. Privately Harry had always considered her the strong one of the marriage and it frightened him to see her like this.

"I had just finished my shower. The first thing I noticed was the smell. Even above the Roger et Gallet. I opened the shower curtain to get a towel…" She stopped to get her breath between the sobs.

"Harry, there was this man, this horrible old man, leering at me, in my own bathroom."

Suddenly she looked up at him. "Where is he?"

"I don't know."

"But you must have passed him on the stairs."

"No."

An awful realisation came over them. "Then he must be still…"

Harry stood up. He looked around for a weapon. The

only thing he could see was the toilet brush. He picked it up. As Morwenna quickly got dressed he searched the many rooms the house contained but found nothing.

They spent a silent morning, jumping at every sound. At lunchtime they went to the pub in Dorstone but Harry did not enjoy the meal. He kept looking suspiciously at the locals, trying to interpret the looks that came his way. Were they involved in this nasty hoax? Were they even more sullen than usual? That outbreak of laughter in the public bar, were they laughing at him?

Even so, they stayed longer in the pub than they normally would. Although the conversation between them was sparse, there was an unacknowledged companionship in being surrounded by other mortals. Coming back to their house as the first early signs of dusk started to darken the sky was not as pleasant as it should have been.

But the house was quiet and innocent. They ate their supper watching what they both dismissively called "the telly" and the mindless noise soothed them. After the problems of the day Morwenna soon fell asleep and Harry sat and watched some pointless outside broadcast thinking about what it had cost the licence payer. So he was the only one who saw, at the back of a crowd of fools who thought a camera was a good opportunity to wave to their mothers, an old, wizened man dressed in brown, slowly waving and mouthing as if making some kind of incantation.

On the Sunday morning Harry had planned to play golf, but when he woke up he could hear torrential rain falling outside. He cursed. The forecast had been for a dry, sunny day.

Eventually he aroused himself enough to get up and draw back the curtains. He looked out on a bright sunny morning with not a cloud in the sky. He stood at the window for a long time, his ears listening to the rain, his eyes looking at the clear sky.

The sound of continually running water disrupted breakfast. Harry turned off the stopcock and searched everywhere but could find no sign of burst pipes or cascading water. He called a few friends, one of whom found a local plumber who would come out to him on a Sunday morning, for a price.

After making a tour of the water system the plumber eventually came down the stairs scratching his head. "Well, it's beaten me. I can't tell where it's coming from. It seems to be coming from all over."

"I'm not paying you for something I already know."

The plumber leaned against the wall in a ruminative sort of way. "You know it's funny. My old granddad used to talk about this house. That's when it was the Mill House."

"You're mistaken. This is the Old Rectory."

"Yes, the last people changed its name just afore they sold it. Reckon they thought they could get a better price for it with a fancy name I shouldn't wonder."

Burbage glowered at him.

"Anyway, the last miller, old Jeremiah Price, he was a bit of a character. Quite a reputation for curing warts and that sort of thing by all accounts, though not the sort you'd want to cross if you take my meaning."

"This has nothing to do…"

"My old grandad came here once over some cut that

wasn't healing and Jeremiah gave him something that worked a treat. While he was here there was a tremendous shower of rain. 'You can't leave while that's on,' said Jeremiah, so my grandad stayed for ages, but the shower kept on until my grandad said he would have to go, rain or not. When he got out of doors it was bone dry and old Jeremiah just laughed and pointed to the mill wheel going around on the stream. 'Course, that can't be your trouble, seeing as the mill wheel was taken out years back, when the stream was blocked off. But my granddad always said that Jeremiah Price was not a body who would go easily to his grave."

A cheque was quickly written and the plumber sent on his way.

The advantage of owning several country houses is that there is always a bed available for you if you need it in an emergency and until you can organise something more suitable in the town.

Harry had not become a millionaire by just sitting back and taking it. He complained. He complained to his local councillor, but the fellow, when he was at last persuaded it was not one of Harry's jokes, said it was outside his mandate. Harry made a resolution to vote Liberal Democrat at the next election and the councillor lost his invitation to Harry's Christmas party where champagne and cottage pie were served, the highlight of the winter season for the more contented part of the Herefordshire elite.

He complained to the Bishop of Hereford, several times, and he was eventually sent a young man who did not wear a dog collar but still claimed to be a priest. The fellow refused to do anything like an exorcism, being more concerned with the feelings of those "on the other side" than he appeared to care about Harry.

Even as a rented property it still did not attract people who were prepared to pay the high monthly rent you would expect for a detached property with fine views, though no one gave a coherent reason why they would not take it.

Eventually, some local people called Price were found by an estate agent who specialised in low-quality lets. They are a large family currently staying with the wife's mother. Now that the rent had come down so steeply, they would be able to afford it.

THE GREAT GODDESS
SEKHMET

Rev Donald Turpin was from what his parishioners called "The North". He was therefore a controversial choice to become a Methodist minister in Hay but in fact his theology translated well from the wet slate roofs of Stockport to the wet slate roofs of Hay. His general view was that most people were going straight to hell and the best thing for his flock was for them to be constantly reminded of the fact. They did not object. The hell-bent carried merrily on their way and the righteous sat there and took it. All was as it should be.

But Donald Turpin was young and ambitious. Deep down, he really worried about the salvation of those in his care and he was prepared to go beyond what was considered right and proper if it ensured their safety. He had made a nuisance of himself in the recently opened betting shop and had the distinction only shared by one sheep farmer from Cusop of being barred from every hostelry in the town. The farmer had at least had the decency to spend a substantial part of his savings before enough became enough. Mr Turpin had never spent a farthing in any pub, but soon after he arrived, had taken to descend on a random establishment on Friday evenings just as the regulars were relaxing. He would declaim, in Bible-College-trained voice, details of just what awaited them when they eventually passed out of the warmth of the pub and into the fires of hell. For some it was a welcome entertainment but the publicans became concerned that it might have some unconscious effect on their flock and universally banned him from their premises. The Anglican vicar, who had been trained at Oxford, gave a sermon on the sin of pride.

No one knows how Mr Turpin came to hear about the Egyptian exhibition. He took no paper and certainly possessed no television. It might have been mentioned on one of the rare occasions he switched on his wireless but most probably it was one of his congregation caught by him in a pastoral visit and desperate to make conversation. To them it was a matter of slight interest, a mere gambit to move the talk away from their immortal soul, but to the reverend it was a sign of Armageddon.

The British Museum was putting on a special exhibition of some of its Ancient Egyptian artefacts. It had so many of them that even top-quality ones were languishing in storage. There was ill feeling back at their place of origin and it had been felt politic to dust some off and make a big thing about them.

For someone steeped in the Old Testament, the Ancient Egyptians were not a neutral concept. Mr Turpin knew very well the pressures that good souls were being put under. That the British Museum, part of the not to be trusted establishment, was doing this could only mean that it was intent on advocating the life of sin and debauchery that such a civilization represented.

Mr Turpin was no coward. He set about organising a day trip to London through a local coach firm that would include stops there and back at respectable cafes and a visit to the exhibition.

He advertised the trip during his sermons over the

next few weeks, making it clear to his congregation that it was their moral duty to attend. In the event only a dozen women signed up. The men, with visions of watching the racing on the telly, Saturday lunchtimes in the pub and other unusual liberties, were quite willing to allow their wives a day of freedom.

The morning of the jaunt proved grey with rain in the air. The youngest on the trip, a shop assistant called Mary Vaughan, took this as a bad sign. Of course she had been away from home before, on holidays with her parents, but these had also been times when her stomach muscles were constantly contracting with imagined horrors. This was worse.

The downward trip to London was uneventful and they entered the dark temple of the British Museum on schedule. Miss Vaughan felt giddy at the size of it and when she entered the Egyptian galleries she felt a terrible sense of dread.

Donald Turpin had done his homework. He strode confidently over to a stone sarcophagus and gathered his twittering charges around it, displacing a couple of American tourists. The women gasped at the mummified body within. Mary felt it a little disrespectful and instead started reading the large notice next to the thing.

"What finer example of the sin of pride than to try to keep your body intact for eternity. If you look closely you can still see wisps of ginger hair. You will recall Esau was a red-headed man. Very close to sin."

Mary never knew what came over her. "It says here

that the hair turns that colour as part of the desiccation process," she said.

Donald looked at her as if it was the first time he had realised she was on the trip. "They would say that," he said and then quickly moved on to another exhibit.

They looked at the wall paintings. The men were just wearing white skirts, while the women, well, they did not sell underwear like that in Hay. "It is a warm country," as someone said, charitably. Donald Turpin was quick to point out that even the aristocratic ladies were wearing diaphanous clothing. The matrons groaned at the thought of having to go out in public in such a revealing costume. Mary thought of appearing in front of Mr Turpin in such a thing. She blushed a very deep red. "They do overheat these places," said old Mrs Price kindly.

Donald led them purposefully towards a large statue at the far end of the room. It was a larger-than-life-size statue of a woman wrapped in a very tight-fitting gown, though, instead of a human head, it had the head of a lioness, even if one wearing standard Egyptian headgear. Mary thought there was something calm and magnificent about the way the head had been carved.

"Now this," said Donald, "is the goddess Sekhmet. She is an aspect of Hathor, the goddess of love."

An appreciative surge went through his audience. Turpin quelled it with a look. "It seems Egyptian gods could never decide what they were really about and always had different aspects. They were changeable and fickle. This is the goddess of love as a destroyer. I ask you, they had so tainted the concept of God's love that they had invented a goddess that they called the lady of terror. They believed that if you only looked into the eyes of the goddess you would be cursed. It seems the Ancient Egyptians were very fond of their cursing."

"A bit like old Bowen at the Whitney Toll," said Mrs Price and the group had a good laugh.

"Now, to show you how empty this all is I want you, in turn, to come before this so called goddess. Gaze into its eyes and see that there is no curse; that this is a lifeless piece of stone."

They dutifully formed a queue and did their minister's bidding. Some glared defiantly, some barely looked, some gave a mock curtsy. Mary, waiting at the end of the line, felt it was like waiting for the vaulting horse in P.E. at school. She had always been a nervous child. Even the bell ringing when someone came into the shop would make her stomach churn.

When it was her turn she dutifully stepped into the glare of the goddess and the other women. Her body was hot and she was only going to glance at the head but when she stood still her eyes rose to the huge blank stare of Sekhmet and, although they were only stone eyes, they seemed to glare right into her. She felt something like an electric charge. Her vision contracted until there were just those eyes. There was a funny buzzing in her ears and then Mrs Price was holding onto her and then Donald Turpin and she was able to regain her footing.

"Let's have a nice cup of tea," said Mrs Price.

On the coach home Mary sat huddled and miserable in her seat. She could not look out of the dark window because, if she did, a pale, disconsolate version of herself would gaze back. Everyone had been very nice to her and that had convinced her that she had disgraced herself. She was sure that the news would get back to her mother. She had never liked being out at night, there seemed always something sinful about it.

She thought she would fall asleep the moment her head hit the pillow, it had been such an eventful day. But, although she had barely been able to keep awake during the preparations for bed, now that she was actually in it her mind was still jazzy with all the events of the day. Within minutes the sheets had become rumpled and uncomfortable and why was it so hot after such a cold day?

She got out of bed and it felt somewhat cooler. Without thinking she took off her nightdress and went back to bed completely naked. The unusual feeling of her body against the sheets shocked her but was not unpleasant. She would just have to wake up before her mother came in with her early morning tea; otherwise there would be more explaining to do.

After a disturbed night of dreams she came wearily down to breakfast on Sunday. She had always considered herself fortunate that she had never been a person who remembered her dreams, but now she was left with a foreboding that was just outside her consciousness. She had been in them, with Sekhmet and a male lion that looked nothing like Lenny the Lion, the ventriloquist's dummy on T.V. Worst of all Donald Turpin had been there. She could not remember any details, perhaps it was just as well, but they had all been fighting or embracing or both, she could not really remember.

She did think about not going to church, but knew that would make people talk. She sat next to her mother trying to be as anonymous as possible. When Donald Turpin strode in wearing his long black cassock she gave a jump that made her mother look at her.

The service passed without too much anxiety. Donald Turpin did go on a bit about their trip to London. There seemed to be a voice in her head that was laughing and saying, "Look at him, he thinks he is so important with his herd of cows that jump to his bidding, but I can tame him."

Then the time she had been dreading, teas and coffees after the service, a time to chat. She had always suspected it was what most of the women came for. She tried to avoid the other members of the expedition and that was why she was in the kitchen on her own when Donald Turpin came in. He said "Good morning," in his normal cheerful way. She could barely nod. He came over to the sink so that he was almost touching her. She imagined that she could feel the heat from his body. He bent down to wash his teacup so that his cheek was right in front of her. She did not think, she just bent down and kissed it. He sprang back, shocked, his cup rolling in the bottom of the sink. She stared back at him, defiant. They were glaring at each other, both angry and shocked.

Sometimes there is grace in sudden acts of outrage. The life of a single minister can be a very lonely one and Mary was extremely pretty. Donald moved forward and they were kissing and Mary felt she was no longer on earth. It was at that moment that Mrs Price, a slow drinker who liked her tea cold, entered the room.

Such scenes are not quickly passed over in a small town. They grow into rumour that become accepted fact and will develop into scandal if the honourable path is not taken. Donald was, at his core, a very honourable man and he found had no wish to relinquish Mary and she had no intention of letting him go. After marriage, he mellowed considerably and was in a good place to steer his congregation through the treacherous waters of the late sixties. In later life, with three fine children at university, Mary sometimes wondered what her life might have been like if she had not taken the risk of that kiss. At the back of her mind she could almost picture the head of a lioness with a glint in its eye and a smile on its face.

THE COBBLER OF
TARRINGTON

David Vernnalls and Sheila Peto were a typical twenties couple. They had both had a pretty bad war, David at Gallipoli, Sheila as a F.A.N.Y. on the Western Front. Afterwards they had determined that life was for living and they were going to do a hell of a lot of it.

One evening in the autumn of 1926 they motored down from Malvern, where they had been refreshing themselves at the spa, to see their new friend Sir Thomas Foley who lived in a fine mansion at Stoke Edith.

The Foleys had made their money from a member of the family being a Speaker of the House of Commons. With the money they had built a fine mansion and both David and Sheila were quite looking forward to some luxurious surroundings after the rigours of the spa.

Sir Thomas Foley was also looking forward to his new young friends arriving. It could get a little dull in the Herefordshire countryside. The young people would spread a bit of London excitement about the place.

He had been expecting them about tea time so was becoming mildly concerned as dusk turned to darkness and they still had not turned up. He was relieved when the butler finally announced them and got up out of his chair to greet them but then stopped when he saw what condition they were in. They looked haggard, their clothes were torn and there was a nasty gash on Miss Peto's forehead.

"Good heavens, what happened to you?"

"I'm really sorry about this. We've had a bit of an

accident," said David with the annoyed insouciance of someone who had been through worse.

After Sheila's cuts had been treated and they had put things right with a cup of tea, David quietly explained their adventure.

"We were a little later leaving Malvern, so we would probably have been abominably late anyway so I apologise for that. Anyway, we had just come through the village of Tarrington and we saw the sharp turning you warned us about coming up, so we knew we were just about there. I was just turning into your drive when some animal or other dashed out of the shrubbery by the gates and seemed to charge the car. I swerved and, I'm afraid, made a bit of a dent in your brick wall."

Sir Thomas was sitting bolt upright, looking very concerned.

"The animal came from the left you say?"

"Why, yes."

"It was a large animal? Larger than a pig but not as big as a deer?"

"Yes, but how did you know?"

"You couldn't be sure what animal it was?"

"No, we couldn't."

Sir Thomas leaned back in his chair.

"It is most unfortunate. I feel to blame. Years ago an ancestor of mine ran over a man there. Ever since he has been trying to kill us just in the manner you describe."

Sir Thomas's visitors sat back in their own chairs, their eyes wide.

After a moment of silence Sir Thomas spoke again.

"I owe you a fuller explanation since you have unfortunately been dragged into the affair. It was some two hundred years ago. My namesake, Sir Thomas Foley, was squire then. Although he was my family I have to say that he was not a good advertisement for money going to young men early in their life. He was spoilt, I think the expression is. Believed that everyone and everything should bow down before him. Naturally he got quite a reputation in the area as not being a man you should cross."

"That sharp bend in the road you mentioned, that I warned you about, that was his creation. Apparently the old road ran straight but old Sir Thomas did not want the hoi polloi going through his land so he built that fine high wall and sent the road around it. People grumbled at the extra distance they had to cover but there was nothing they could do about it in those days.

"One night he was coming back very late and, just as the coach turned in to go through the gates, there was an almighty bump that knocked Sir Thomas clear onto the floor. You can imagine that the language he devoted to the coachman would have made the groom blush. When they took a look at what had caused the trouble they found they had run over old George Bedford, the cobbler of Tarrington. What the old boy had been doing there it was too late to know for sure but he was known to spend most of his evenings in the Tarrington Arms. Presumably he had mistaken his way home and lain down to rest at a most unfortunate spot.

"Sir Thomas cursed and got back in the coach. He demanded the coachman carry on to the house. The coachman promised to come back to see that the old man's body was treated properly but Sir Thomas told him in no uncertain terms that his first duty was to take care of the horses and, since he wanted to be off hunting at first light, he did not want the grooms up all night on some foolishness. That idiot, who had had the stupidity to fall asleep in the middle of the road, was past all care anyway.

"So it was that poor George lay out on the road all night. It was only when Sir Thomas had been safely set off hunting that his servants could go and carry the body back to his home and proper respects paid to it.

"It was a few days later, the night after George Bedford's funeral, that Sir Thomas was next coming back late at night in his coach. It was just taking the turn into the gates where, only a few days before, it had run over the cobbler, when the horses screamed and swerved, dashing themselves into the brick wall and taking the coach with them so that it smashed itself against the wall and fell over on its side.

"Sir Thomas came out of the crash with barely more cuts and bruises than you yourself sustained, as did the coachman but one of the horses had broken its leg and had to be destroyed. Sir Thomas was mad at the loss to himself and blamed the coachman for taking the bend too fast. But the coachman forever maintained that, approaching the gates, something, larger than a pig but smaller than a deer, had jumped out at them, scaring the horses and making them swerve. It was his opinion that the horses were calm beasts and would not have been frightened by anything natural. There was something devilish in the thing that had attacked them.

"Whatever the cause, and there was plenty of talk about it in the Tarrington Arms, the same phenomenon occurred several more times within Sir Thomas's lifetime, although he eventually died in his bed. But his death did not end the visitations, if such they be. Every so often it happens again. I'm sorry that you had to be inconvenienced by it."

The London couple remained silent, each vowing that they, in the future, would remain in town and never trouble the countryside again. They stayed the night and then discovered some urgent business that meant they must leave the following day.

Three years later, in the bad winter of 1929, David rushed into Sheila's bedroom early one morning carrying a copy of that day's *Times*. On an inside page there was a short article to which he urgently pointed. It was a short description of a terrible fire that had broken out at the mansion of Stoke Edith in the County of Herefordshire. No one knew how it had started but, because of the exceptionally cold weather, when the fire brigade had eventually arrived, they found the water frozen so they were unable to prevent the house and all its treasure from being destroyed. David and Sheila looked at each other. Perhaps something had got tired of occasional lunges and had tried a more direct approach. A few years later they told the story to their friend Daphne de Maurier. I believe she used the idea in her novel *Rebecca* for the burning down of Mandalay.

If you travel from Ledbury to Hereford you will go through that tight bend at Stoke Edith. If you pass it in darkness you may feel slightly eerie, knowing the story as you do now. But if you pass it in daylight occasionally you will find the brick wall in need of repair, where a car did not quite manage the bend… for some reason.

THE POT OF GOLD

One afternoon, on his way back from Madley School, Fred Hamer found a gold sovereign on the ground. He quickly picked it up and thought it was his lucky day. Perhaps he was wrong.

Forever after that he kept his eyes on the ground wherever he went in the hope of finding another one. He never did, but he found quite a few coppers and a reasonable amount of silver.

After he had finished his schooling he found a job in a bank. He enjoyed the feeling of money passing through his hands even though the coins and notes were not his own. Because that was what he appreciated about the job he refused all invitations to rise in the bank, preferring to remain as a clerk where, every day, he was handling money. As the years passed he was pointed out as an eccentricity. Rumours grew up that he could have risen to the very top and have a good house in London if he had chosen. He was often used as a warning by his superiors to young clerks as the example of a lack of ambition.

He walked into Hereford every day from Madley and every night back again, always with his eyes searching the ground for a glint of coin. His heart rose if he found even a penny. If, as was more common, he returned home without luck he was miserable all evening. It was a wonder to nobody that he never married.

What coins he collected and the money left over from his salary, which was substantial since his needs were few, he exchanged for gold sovereigns. What he did with these was a mystery. The assumption was that he kept them at his lodgings and cackled over them every evening in the traditional way of the miser. It was another source of ill feeling with his superiors, that he did not appear to trust to the safety of the bank, but preferred to keep his savings under the mattress or whatever else he did with it.

Given his continual downcast posture, by the age of thirty he had developed a noticeable stoop. By his fifties he was badly bent over, so that he could barely look at his customers over the counter, regarding them with a disconcerting, suspicious glower through his thick eyebrows.

One hot summer's evening he was walking back home as usual, scouring the road for money. Wearing his thick three-piece suit of winter weight (he saw only the need for the one suit and decided that a warm coat was generally of more use) and carrying his overcoat in case of rain, he was feeling hot and uncomfortable. He was through the village of Clehonger and almost home but took no consolation from that, since he had found no money for three weeks. There was a pain in his shoulder that was coming to such a pitch that he was having trouble in concentrating on the ground in front of him. So much so that he had to stop and lean on a wall. He tried to straighten himself but that only made the pain worse.

After what he determined was a sufficient rest, though it had seemed to make little difference to the pain, he set off on his way again. As soon as he stepped out the pain shifted to the centre of his chest and rose in intensity. Mr Hamer staggered and fell. His body convulsed in pain, but that seemed to him that that part was already a long way away. What most struck him was the blue of the sky. How beautiful. He realised with a pang of regret that it was a very long time since he had last noticed it. As his body shivered in its final death throes, Fred Hamer realised what he had missed.

He was not particularly mourned, old misers rarely are. What most interested people was the whereabouts of all the gold sovereigns that he had amassed over his lifetime. A search was made by the authorities of his house but nothing was found, not even a will that might have given a clue to some long-lost relative or sweetheart for whom he might have been saving them.

Mysterious holes appeared in his garden overnight but, since no resident of Madley suddenly decamped to the South of France, it was assumed that the gold had not been found.

Time passed and other things came to the fore in the conversations of the people of Madley, although this topic did still occasionally resurface when other matters lapsed.

Then a figure in black started appearing. It was always seen a long way off and at first no one paid much heed to it. Then someone mentioned how much it looked like old Fred. Suddenly there was interest. An old codger was found in the snug bar of the pub who was of the opinion that misers cannot rest while their hoard remains undiscovered. Clearly Fred Hamer was trying to communicate the location of the gold.

The previously quiet night-time streets of Madley were soon thronged with people, all anxious to be the one to whom Fred imparted this valuable piece of information. Such congestion is not the ideal place for a ghost but still there were occasional sightings but, if anyone got close or called after the spectre, it vanished completely, leaving the individual regretting their missed opportunity.

Gradually the public interest waned. The years went by and Fred and his treasure were forgotten. If any spectres made their appearance, the reason was forgotten or perhaps people were not very observant any longer and did not notice anything out of the ordinary.

Eventually Fred's old house was rented to a local family by the name of Phillips. Bob worked at a light-metal factory in Hereford. It was a repetitious sort of job but Bob did not greatly mind it. The wages were not great but neither were the responsibilities.

His wife, Beryl, was not of the same opinion. With three kids and an ever-rising food and clothing bill, she was forever onto Bob to better himself and bring more money into the house. Bob, in deference to his wife, had no hobbies that would further drain the family coffers, other than membership of a local football team that played in a lowly league in town on a Saturday afternoon. His best friend and fellow full back, John Brooke, used to rib Bob that he was under Beryl's thumb. Bob took the jokes in good part. In contrast to Bob, who was content with the lower leagues, John thought that he himself was Division One material, if not in football then in life.

After one game, when Bob looked especially downtrodden, John suggested a solution. It so happened that John was dissatisfied with his lodgings at the moment, the landlady objecting to the hours he kept. Why not John becoming a paying guest at the Phillips's? Surprisingly to Bob, Beryl accepted the idea, money is money after all, and the arrangement worked reasonably well. John was out most evenings, a bachelor, free and easy, Beryl had more to make ends meet and Bob got fewer tongue lashings.

A few months after John had moved in, he was spending the night in, being temporarily short of funds and Beryl had been careful to get her money in advance. Bob was leafing through the *Hereford Times* when his eye was caught by a picture of their house.

"Hey, look at this!" he cried to John. Forced into it, John started reading the article in an off-hand way but then grabbed the paper from Bob.

"There used to be a miser living here and they never found his stash of gold," he said excitedly and then seemed suddenly to think better of it. "There's probably nothing in it." To Bob's disappointment John seemed unwilling to take the discussion any further.

That night Beryl was woken by strange noises downstairs. Bob was disinclined to investigate, assuring her it was nothing. In the morning, when John was asked if he had heard anything, he laughed and said, "It's probably old Fred Hamer's ghost come back."

A few days later Bob was having his Saturday morning lie in. He was vaguely aware of Beryl getting up and he thought of the bacon and eggs to come. Then he heard his wife scream.

Hurriedly putting on his dressing gown, he rushed downstairs. Beryl was standing in the kitchen. One of the kitchen cupboards had been wrenched off the wall and a large hole made in the brickwork, disclosing an empty cavity. The back door, that should have been locked, was wide open.

Bob trudged next door to wake his neighbours, so he could use their telephone to call the police. It was only when two constables had arrived, examined the kitchen and then asked if anyone else lived in the house, that Bob and Beryl thought of John. His room was empty. Bob assumed that he must be working a Saturday shift and forgotten to tell them, but Beryl was not so sure. The constables lost interest when the couple were unable to confirm that anything was missing.

John did not return that night. In fact neither Bob nor Beryl ever saw him again. Beryl naturally put two and two together and blamed John for the desecration of her kitchen. Bob, although he did not confide in Beryl, wondered if old Fred Hamer might have something to do with it as well.

HOW TO DEAL WITH GHOSTS

(A tribute to Andrew Haggard,
a lover of the Herefordshire dialect.)

Ted and George were hard at their work one day then the Gov'nor stopped for a word. It being close on Halloween the conversation turned to ghosts.

"How about you Ted? Did you ever see a ghost?"

"Can't mind that I have, but I heard on a couple."

There was a pause and it looked like Ted was going to start work again. "You can't leave it like that, can he George?"

George gazed into the distance and showed no inclination to get back to the job. "Come on, what's the story?"

"Well, it ain't no story neither, but it was when I was a boy. They laid 'un in Amstell Pond."

"How did they get the ghost into it?"

"Why, the parson read her small and put her in a matchbox and throwed her into it."

"The ghost of a woman then."

"Oh yes. Her was the first wife of Hodges as used to have the blacksmithing at Acton Cross."

"Well, what happened?"

"That Mrs Hodges dies and leaves two children, and the blacksmith he marries again and very quick he did it too, weren't that so George?"

"Ah!"

"And her was bad to the children of the first wife. And so the first wife's spirit took to coming back to her children, protecting 'em like, not terrifying them but just standing at their beds. Just in her proper clothes, not her shroud, which might have terrified 'em. But she came so regular that word got out and all the place was talking on it. And second wife won't take any more of it so she tells parson and gets him to lays 'un and afterwards parson says he don't never want no such job again, fair made him sweat it did. Old Copeland was the parson then. He had to get eleven other parsons so there was twelve on 'em each with a lit candle. First they has to raise her 'cos with spirits you got to raise 'un afore you falls 'un. And she wasn't of a mind to leave her children so she gives them all kind of trouble, all the candles going out 'til there was only one candle left and fortunate that candle kept burning else she'd a bested 'em. And they got reading her smaller and smaller and got her real small and pushed 'un in a matchbox and throwed 'un in Amstell Pond as I was telling you, and her aren't troubled no one since, ent that so George?"

"Ah!"

"Seems a bit harsh. She was only looking out for her children."

"That might be so, but you don't want to be messing with any spirits. That's my view anyway."

"What was the other ghost?"

"That was over at Avenbury Church. It's haunted all right. There was two brothers lived near the church, at Brookhouse. The one, he were a good chap and a used to play the organ in the church regular like. Everybody liked 'un. T'other he were a sclem, right good for nothing, never did no work, and was allus a-bothering his brother for money and such. Nobody couldn't suffer 'un. How it came to happen I don't rightly know, but I expect it was over some gambling debt that the waste of space had gotten for hisself. By this time the younger brother had grown resentful at his brother's good luck and could not see that his own misfortune was all of his own making. One evening this brother hears the old organ playing right beautiful so he knows his brother is practising. He lies in wait for him on the water bridge over the prill just off the Bromyard road. The organist, I imagine his heart fell when he saw what was waiting for him, he had got tired of this drain on his purse. This time there was no, "Here you are then," but the other brother was desperate and it ended up coming to blows. The good-for-nothing brother, he was stronger and angrier, and he picks up a stone from the river bank and gives his brother such a blow that it kills him. Of course he then high tails it off to Australia or some such place before they can catch him. But that weren't the end of it, not by no manner of means, for arter that the organ used to play nights and no lights nor nobody there. There's many still alive that's heard it.

"That came to be the talk of the place, and presently that come on so powerful the parson he say he must fall the ghost. So, one day, at the same time as the murdering, he comes to the bridge all in his religious clothes and he lights three candles and he starts to pray and presently the one candle, that flickered and went out. The parson he prays harder but it weren't no good for the second candle, that went out too.

"Then the parson he prays that hard till the sweat fair ran off his nose and the third candle, that started to gutter but the parson kept on a praying and just when it looked like it would go out it suddenly come up bright again, and just so well it did as if it had a gone out the ghost would have bested him.

"That didn't stop the music altogether, but the pain seemed to have gone out of it and them as lived about there learned not to take a lot of notice, but strangers wouldn't go near the place after dark, and, if they heard it, well, they got terrified.

"'Cos I don't think that parson did as good a job as Mr Copeland. It's not something to take on, on your own. Those spirits, they gets their own back. Now there are times when the bell of the church tolls of its own accord, with no Christian near it. That is a sign that the vicar of Avenbury will not last out the night. I should judge that that scares 'un when 'em hears that late at night. Don't you think so George?"

"Ah!"

THE HOARWITHY
ROMEO

Harry Watkins was a lady's man. At least that is how he liked to think of himself. For others, especially fathers of daughters in the village of Hoarwithy, he was a damned nuisance that somebody ought to take a shotgun to.

Certainly he was lucky in his chosen hobby, although not a handsome man. In a beauty contest with the other men of the village he would have become the owner of a nice new wooden spoon and a cracked mirror. But he had a confidence about him that many of the more handsome men in the village lacked. A man of confidence, with six sisters at home, therefore had a considerable advantage.

At the time of our story, he had at least two acknowledged illegitimate children in the village and the surrounding areas and there were a few others that mysteriously shared his bright blue eyes. One would have thought that would irretrievably damage him in any right-thinking lady's eyes, but for many, it only seemed to act as a means of encouragement, they would be the one who would tame him.

At that time his eyes were on a young woman called Lily Morris. He only ever had one quarry at any one time; he was, in his own way, a man of principle. She was not the most obvious target. Some might call her prim and not mean it in a good way, something to do with the thick spectacles she wore, but Harry had never seen such a thing as an obstacle. Once he had set his sights on her he made every effort to be in her vicinity at all moments that he could, despite the long hours he had to work as a farm labourer, and she also spent long hours working in the village post office of Much Birch. But she did spend her Sundays at the village chapel. Harry was not a chapel man himself, but he was not a man afraid of making the necessary sacrifices. So he was there at the next Sunday tea that the Methodists had arranged, making polite conversation with the old ladies and learning more than he ever wanted to about missionary work in Nyasaland. He was careful not to give his name. This far out of his usual haunts they might not know his face but they might well know his reputation. As he suspected they were happy to see him, not many men under forty came to these things so he had the advantage of being an oddity. However Lily seemed mostly to be involved in getting the tea ready, then serving it, then washing up so, for most of the afternoon, he had to control a desperate urge to run amok with a scythe.

At the end of the afternoon he was rewarded. He saw that she was preparing to depart and, leaving one old lady in mid sentence, rushed after her, making it appear that he was just happening to be leaving at the same time.

"Good afternoon, wasn't it," he ventured.

"What?"

"Good way of passing a Sunday afternoon."

"I find them a little boring. My mother thinks it's good for me to do it."

From then on their meetings continued to happen by chance over the next few weeks, until he felt he knew her well enough.

So, one evening, "Fancy going to the Hoarwithy dance this Saturday?"

"Oh, that's very kind, but I'm going out with someone."

This was such a total shock to him that he stopped dead.

"Who on earth?"

"Rob Jacobs."

"The postman?"

"Yes."

Harry had not had a rival before. He had avoided them. He could not think what to do.

"I see. Thank you."

He let her walk away from him, cursing himself at how weak he sounded. Yet he did not fancy the idea of just walking away and finding somebody else. He had sat through all that Methodist twaddle for heaven's sake. With his record he was sure he could be competitive if he tried.

His job meant early starts, so he was used to seeing the postman going around the place. He had not really thought of him before. Now he looked. He was a weedy little man. Harry could not believe it. How could anyone choose that over him?

In the Harp one night he saw Rob drinking. He was on his own.

"So, you going out with Lily Morris?"

Rob blinked irritatingly. "We have an understanding."

"Well bloody well stop understanding. I've got my eye on her."

"You! You're not fit for her to stand on, let alone talk to."

Harry never considered himself a violent man. It was just the way this silly little man blinked at him. He knew better than to do something straight away and get himself barred. He just walked away, angry to think that Rob must have thought he had got one over on him. But one has to be disciplined to be a great lover.

It was a fine evening so he just waited down the lane, around the corner from the pub. Rob was not a noted drinker so he did not have to wait long and Harry saw the figure he had been waiting for. Rob had his head down and did not notice Harry behind the hedge as he walked past. Harry chuckled to himself and walked out onto the path behind the postman.

Rob walked fast, probably something to do with his profession, so that Harry had to jog to catch up with him. In doing so he stood on a dead twig, which cracked loudly under his weight. Rob turned around at the noise. Harry enjoyed the look of surprise and concern on his features.

"What do you want?"

"Thought I might change your mind for you."

"And how are you going to do that?"

Harry lunged at Rob and caught him on the chin with his fist. Rob staggered but did not fall. Instead he raised his fists and squared up to Harry. Both thought of Lily in her glasses and then charged into each other.

The fight was swift and furious, but Harry was the bigger man and soon that began to tell. Rob went down on all fours and Harry kicked him hard in the head. Rob slumped to the ground.

For a while Harry regarded his former opponent with a smirk on his face.

"Now then, you going to leave Lily Morris alone?"

Rob did not say anything. Harry cursed. He was

going to have to wait around until the fellow regained consciousness. It was already starting to get dark and he would have an early start tomorrow. He kicked the fallen man's legs almost gently. He was surprised by how unresisting they were.

It came into his mind that Rob was not shaming.

"Come on, get up," he said angrily. There was still no response. If anything the postman seemed even limper than the last time he kicked him.

"Get up damn you!" There was a note of fear in his voice now. When the postman stopped joking he was going to get another good basting.

Perhaps there should not be blood coming out of his ears and his head was at a funny angle.

"Rob, come on lad." Harry was bending down over the fallen figure, shaking him by the shoulders. Rob was as limp as ever.

A shiver ran down Harry's spine and he clutched at his throat as if thinking of the hangman's noose.

"This can't be," he said, hoping that, if he said it, it would make it true.

But shaking was not going to bring back the postman to his familiar rounds. After a while this awful truth penetrated Harry's brain and he stopped shaking the lifeless corpse.

He stood up and regarded it, almost objectively. He could just go home. No one would connect him with this. Yet they must have seen him in the pub earlier. The police would want to talk to him and they would not be slow in inventing a motive. As far as he knew the postman had no other enemies. He would be the one the police would come for. They always came for someone, guilty or not.

Much better if the body were never found. He had heard somewhere that if there was no body the police could not charge you with murder. He looked around him. He could drop the body behind the hedge, but the farmer would find it and hordes of flies would find it first. There was a pond nearby. If he weighted the body down into the mud at the bottom it would probably stay down there long enough. But ponds get drained and bodies fill with gas and rise. Better get rid of it the way you get rid of any other body, bury it.

He could not do it now. He had no spade and there was a terrible lethargy creeping over him and he just wanted to sleep.

He could not sleep yet. He bent down again and, with what seemed to him some super-human effort, picked up the body and carried it to the other side of the hedge. He did not like the dull thud it made as he dropped it on the ground but he could not help that. It would be safe enough there for a day he reckoned. If not it was just too bad.

He felt better the next morning. He had slept surprisingly well and was pleased with himself for having such a strong constitution. His employer noted with what a will he scythed the thistles that afternoon. Then he waited for the darkest part of the night and returned to where he had left the postman.

It is surprisingly difficult to dig a grave when you are not used to it and doing it in the dark. Harry knew he had to go deep to stop the foxes digging the body up again. But he was a good workman and just kept going steadily. By the time he heard the first birds he felt he was deep enough. It did not take so long to drop the body into the pit and fill it with soil. Then it was time to go to work with tales of drunken excess for his workmates in order to excuse his tiredness.

People miss a postman and the news of the strange disappearance was soon going around the neighbourhood. Harry thought he would go and console Lily.

"Oh Mr Watkins, isn't it terrible."

Harry moved to put his arms around her in a consoling sort of way. She moved quickly away from him.

"Mr Watkins! How could you?"

"He's gone. He's left you. He's not worthy of you."

She looked at him and Harry was shocked to see pity in her eyes. He was expecting anger. He could work with anger.

"Why he has gone and where he has gone I don't know. But I know him Mr Watkins and I know he has a good reason. I intend to wait for him."

He looked at her incredulously. "You can't waste your life on someone who won't come back to you."

"You can't know that."

Harry bit his lip in frustration. She started to move away from him. He wanted to call after her but he was fearful of what he might say so stayed rooted to the spot.

Time went on as it always does. Harry's eye strayed quite soon. Perhaps he wanted to put the past behind him. Not so Lily. She never went out with a man again, never put herself in danger of it, confining her social life to Methodist teas and Post Office get-togethers, neither of which were likely to put her in the way of temptation.

Inevitably some woman got her hooks into Harry and married him. He found he was not too horrified. He was tired. He had a couple of fine sons and his employer evidently thought enough of him to find him a cottage. It was as good a life as he could hope for, yet, every time he caught sight of Lily something like a knife went through him. It was not regular, he kept out of Much Birch, but every so often, about once a year, he would see her and he would feel the shock again.

It was the season of threshing. Harry, one of the oldest and experienced workers, was on the top of the machine, feeding the stooks onto the belt. It was hot, dangerous work.

It was Lily's day off. She had heard there was a poor old lady in Hoarwithy who was not long for this world. She thought she ought to visit her. She had no other motive.

Harry was thinking that he ought to call for a break. The heat and the noise were making him feel dizzy. He looked up to see how many more stooks were being thrown up to him by his underlings, just as Lily was passing along the lane. He felt that sharp lurch in his stomach, his right foot slipped on some corn that had dropped from his fork. Before he could think much about it he had overbalanced and was in the blades of the threshing machine.

Lily was thinking of Rob as she walked along the lane. She did not think of him every day now but, with the mindlessness of walking, the thought had come to her. Subconsciously she had heard the sound of the threshing machine but paid it no mind. She had not even glanced at it. When the sound deepened and the machine growled as if full to bursting and people started shouting she did not bother looking back.

More years went by and Harry's sons grew up. The eldest, also called Harry, had taken his father's death hard. It was not so much losing the cottage and having to move out of the district to stay with his mother's family. It was the pointlessness of his father's death that had left a gulf in his soul.

He had just turned twenty when he managed to find a job back in Hoarwithy. It pleased him that he could go regularly into the pub that his father used to frequent. He went every evening that he still had wages in his pocket.

He was coming back late one dark night humming a song to himself, happy enough. He heard something padding on the metal of the road behind him and looked round. There was a big black dog lopping up towards him. It stopped when he stopped.

"Get away you black beast." Harry was not frightened; he just did not want the creature near him. He picked up a stone and threw it at the dog. It hit the creature hard on the flank but the dog did not flinch, it did not run off, it just kept looking at him so that Harry had no choice but to look into the dog's eyes.

Then Harry turned and he ran. He ran until he came to the cottage he shared with his brother, bursting through the door just as his brother was heading up to bed.

"What's the matter with you?"

"Nothing. There's nothing the matter."

"Doesn't look like it."

"Shut yer mouth. There's nothing wrong with me."

The next few nights Harry spent at home rather than going to the pub as usual, several times almost coming to blows with his brother on being questioned on this. But a young man's brain is resilient, especially where alcohol is concerned and on the Saturday night he was back in the pub.

A certain sobriety hit him with the chill wind when he came out of the pub late that night, but he reasoned that the dog was not likely to be there a second time and that he had imagined the worst of it.

All was well until he was just getting out of the village when he heard that familiar pad, pad of clawed feet behind him. He did not want to turn round but he had to. There was the dog. Harry could not help looking into those eyes.

"What you want?" he found himself saying, petrified that the dog would reply.

Instead the dog ran off but only a few yards. Harry tried to go the other way, but the dog growled deep in his throat.

"Alright yer bugger." Harry stood still.

The dog ran off, stopped and looked back. Harry walked after him and the dog ran off again, stopping after a few yards to make sure Harry was following.

So they went on for a mile or so out of the village until the dog came to a hedge. It stopped, its ears back, its body shaking. Whatever was over the other side of the hedge, if it was frightening that dog, Harry had no wish to see it. He took a step back and the dog growled at him.

The dog behind him, Harry walked to the gate and

looked into the field. It was empty. There was a flash of movement beside him and the dog jumped over the gate and ran to the corner of the hedge near where they had been standing. It started digging, a terrible whine coming from its throat.

Harry walked over to the dog. It stopped and watched him and then started digging again with a new ferocity. Harry bent down and started digging as well. A thought came into his mind of one of the rare times he had helped his father in their cottage garden, digging together like this.

His hands hit something hard. He wiped the soil away from it. It was bone. He wiped a bit more and saw it was a skull. The dog leaped away and lay down some five yards away, whining.

Harry took to his heels. He ran to the police house. Eventually he persuaded a sleepy policeman to come with him to the field. When the policeman saw the skull he woke up pretty quickly and did what any policeman would do in the circumstances, he arrested Harry. Harry tried to explain about the dog, but there was no dog to be seen.

After a few days in the cells, the experts who had now dug up the body decided that it had been in the ground longer than Harry had been on the earth. One clue to the identity of the corpse was three GPO buttons found by the body.

When Lily heard the news a broad smile spread on her face. The smile was still on her face when she died a few weeks later. The woman who came to lay her out said it was unusual to see such a smile on the face of a spinster.

Harry, though released from the police cells, did not long survive. There were no more jokes and laughter. People made up their own reasons for his decline but the real reason, which Harry would only tell his brother on his deathbed, concerned the eyes of the dog he had seen. He was convinced, and went to his grave convinced, that the dog had looked at him with the bright blue eyes of his dead father.

LITTLE EMMA

Emma was fourteen. Her father, Thomas Foulger, was the successful tenant farmer of Aylton Court near Ledbury. It was a life almost without care and Emma seemed to understand how lucky she was. She was the most serene and placid of creatures, the sort of girl with whom even maiden aunts did not mind being in the same room. She never teased her brothers, always finished her meal without having to be warned about those less fortunate than herself and skipped along the lanes near her home, increasing the joy of all who met her. She was never back later than the time her mother had placed upon her.

Her younger brother, Henry, was just of an age when he could be allowed to enter the world of men; he was going to go on his first shooting expedition. Emma listened as her father gave him a stern talk in the parlour the night before. The oil lamps seemed to gleam with a baleful yellow light that evening, almost like the times she had a fever, as she listened to all the things that could go wrong and all the things the boy must remember to do. There seemed so many things that could go wrong and lead to death or terrible injury that Emma felt her stomach grow heavy with foreboding.

For someone who normally fell asleep as soon as her head hit her pillow she spent a restless night and had trouble with her breakfast. Her mother concluded that she was ill and insisted she go back to her room and rest.

But she could not read or find any other way to distract herself. At every crack of the distant guns she jumped and then waited nervously for the next. At last a long silence came. Still she was tense, nervously waiting for the next explosion. As nothing came she went to the window. There were her father and brother just walking into the farmyard, smiles on their faces. Everything must have gone well.

She rushed out of her bedroom and along the landing. With less of the decorum she devoted to coming down the stairs she bounded down and was just reaching the last flight as the front door opened and her brother entered.

Every sportsman knows that, when you have a gun in your hand, there are only two things you should ever concentrate on, your gun and the thing you are going to shoot with it. Henry was young; seeing his beloved sister coming down the stairs and with so much he wanted to tell her, he too rushed to meet her, tripped on the mat and the gun went off.

These were the days before safety catches or double barrels that could be broken. The shot caught Emma full in the chest. She was knocked over and slid down the remainder of the stairs.

The loud explosion in the confined space of the hall brought her parents, siblings and servants running, apart from Henry who cowered by the grandfather clock, unable to take in the nightmare that was happening.

Emma remained with a surprised expression on her face as if unable to take in the cries all around her. She was dead within minutes.

The terrible news quickly spread and there was not a house in the parish that did not feel touched by the tragedy.

A terrible gloom covered the fields and lanes as people thought about Emma, how she had cheered them when they met her and now they would never see her again.

So it was a large crowd that gathered three days later for the funeral. Aylton is a small church, and the churchyard as well as the church was soon full of people who had come to pay their respects, giving what little comfort they could give to a family that had been torn apart. After the brief committal service Emma's small coffin was placed in the good red Herefordshire earth and the churchyard left to its usual tranquillity.

This would have remained one of many small tragedies enacted over the land, soon forgotten or suddenly recalled many years later with a shake of the head but for the worse things that occurred next.

Two days after the funeral a farm labourer, on his dawn walk to work, casually glanced into the churchyard and saw there was something wrong. Although it might make him late he went through the gate and over to the site of Emma's grave. Instead of the mound of earth the grave was open, the earth cast all over the place. Worse, there was no sign of the coffin.

It was clear to everyone what had happened. It was the work of the resurrectionists… grave robbers… body-snatchers. These were the days of science when doctors, not unreasonably, wanted to find out how the body worked. But these were also the days when it was illegal to use the body of a human being for anatomy teaching, unless it was the body of a murderer or a suicide, and there were just not enough of those to go about. There is always somebody who will fill a gap in the market, in this case digging up the recently deceased and selling them to a doctor or medical school who was not going to ask too many questions as to how they acquired such a thing.

Reluctantly the family had to be told and you can imagine how much it added to their suffering. Not just that no one wants that to happen to their child but also, in those days, people believed literally in the resurrection of the dead. When the last trump came the graves would open and the body ascend to heaven in whatever condition it had been put there in the first place. If your body was scattered all over the place, with some of it still in jars, what hope did you have?

To think that he would not see his beloved daughter in heaven drove Mr Thomas Foulger to distraction. He wrote to all the medical schools in the country pleading for the return of the body. None replied, which might not come as any surprise. It is not a thing that you would want to own up to.

But Mr Foulger did see his daughter again. He was coming in at the front door one day when, out of the corner of his eye, he saw the familiar little figure skipping down the stairs. When he turned to look the stairs were empty. He sat down at the bottom of them and wept.

It was no surprise to the country people that Emma's ghost should be abroad after all that had happened to her. It is never good luck to see a ghost so people started to be a bit wary of walking the lanes near Aylton Court. But those that did see her reported that she was not the vengeful ghost that she had every right to be. Instead, they saw her picking flowers, smiling and generally behaving in the same blithe way she had done when she was alive.

She has even been seen in Aylton churchyard. If you have a mind to it you can go and see her empty grave which is still there, at the back of the church, close to the wall. Be polite if you see her because she will do you no harm.

THE TEMPTATION OF
LADY TEMPEST

Henry Lambert was a happy man. He was as honest as he needed to be and still sleep soundly in his big feather bed. He was as devious as the world required him to be, devious enough to have done well in the turbulent financial markets of the mid-eighteenth century. He had also done well in the marriage market, securing Jane Pritchard, the heiress to the Hope End estate near Colwall in the county of Hereford. Few taxes, profitable wars and a compliant workforce, there was no better time to be a country gentleman. He was a happy man and many envied him. That was until he became a widower and the father of a daughter, all in one night.

But life has to go on. The girl had brought him misery but, despite that, he made sure that her bringing up was all that it should be, even if he could not help being a little distant with the child. By 1790, the daughter, Sarah, had grown up into a twenty-four-year-old heiress; a little plain by the standards of London society and also very innocent of the ways of the world. Her father valued her, as he would an estate that he did not often visit but was still something he did not want to lose. He kept her a little too shut off from polite society for her to know how wicked people could be. She had really only known good, straightforward, Herefordshire folk.

But a fortune is a fortune and the existence of this little innocent was well known in such quarters that cared about such things. One who cared particularly was Sir Henry Tempest, a Yorkshire baronet. He had inherited the family fortune only a few years before but had now spent all of it on gambling and loose living. He did not regret a penny. Being the fifth baronet he could not just go out and get a job. There was clearly only one alternative. The current stocks of heiresses in London were terrible hard work and their brothers too quick to suggest the diversion of a duel to sort out the matter. The more he thought of the mysterious Sarah Pritchard-Lambert the more attractive a proposition she became.

He decided she was at least worth a trip out of London by way of reconnaissance. The coach trip to Colwall was ghastly but the inn was decent enough. He stayed downstairs in the evening, buying anyone who came in a drink and pontificating on the terrible events over in France, much to the locals' amusement and enlightenment.

Eventually, the talk came around to Miss Sarah of Hope End. He learnt that she had a face that would not curdle the milk but neither would it bring out the sun on a cloudy day. "Ah well," he thought: "I can always blow out the candle on the wedding night."

More of interest to him was the fact that Miss Sarah was considered "Right innocent like," and too easily taken in by superstitious country ways than someone of her class should be. He also learnt that the next day was market day and Miss Sarah, as like as not, would be around the village doing whatever small marketing interested her.

How a young aristocrat acquired the clothes of a gipsy woman it is probably better not to enquire. Suffice it to say that there was one gypsy lass who came back to the camp early that morning wearing better clothes than she started out with.

Sir Henry, looking a more convincing gipsy girl than a Yorkshire baronet has any right to, wandered around the market barely noticed but with his eyes as sharp as a hunter's.

At last he spotted her, a girl in her early twenties, better dressed than any other woman on Colwall Green and with a carefree expression on her face that annoyed him.

He waited for her to walk near him and then sidled up.

"Tell your fortune young miss?"

She jumped, being unaware that there was a gipsy standing behind her left shoulder.

"Let me foretell your future, dearie."

Before she could stop the creature it had taken hold of her hand and was gazing at it intently.

As far as Sir Henry was concerned it was a little pudgier than he would have liked, but beggars cannot be choosers as he knew only too well.

"Ah, a fine hand. I see a good marriage to a handsome young gentleman."

Sarah laughed. Gipsies always said this sort of thing. But she was not displeased.

"And your good fortune is about to be realised. If you were only to go to Colwall church at eleven o'clock tomorrow morning you will meet the man who will be your true love."

Sarah's heart fluttered. Gipsies were not usually so specific in their predictions. She thanked the woman for her trouble and gave her a silver coin which was pocketed with alacrity.

That evening Sarah was much more distracted than

she knew she ought to be. Part of her thought it was all foolery but gipsies had a certain reputation for being able to see things that were not given to house dwellers. By the morning she had decided. What harm could there be in just going to the church at the appointed time and seeing what transpired?

So, at eleven o'clock that day, she found herself near Colwall churchyard. She expected to see it empty or worse, some oafish farmer's son that she would recognise. If it was she would jolly well turn around and come home. True love or not her romantic imagination was determined to do better than a farmer for a husband.

But she was wrong, there was no one she knew in the churchyard, only an elegantly-dressed young man who was strutting around as if he had a poker down his shirt, glancing at the church with an arrogance that told the world he had seen much better on the Grand Tour.

Her legs went to water, but she had come this far, she could not retreat now. The lychgate creaked abominably as she came through it, then she was at a loss as to what to do. She could not approach a male stranger. As things turned out she need not have worried. At the sound of the gate the man had turned and then stood still, as if transfixed. Suddenly remembering himself he took off his hat and bowed low, which Sarah took to be a London custom.

"Forgive me. It was rude of me to stare so but I could not help myself. In London we rarely see such honest beauty."

It was not long before Sarah discovered that this was no less than a baronet, come to take the waters at Malvern but, bored, had wandered off the usual fashionable trails to this little church. He had not expected to see anything that caught his eye but how wrong he had been. Their meeting was short but the young man had pressed her to meet him again. She was happy to agree.

For a fortnight they had regular meetings that her father was unaware of until she came to him one evening to say that Sir Henry Tempest was to call on him the next day to ask for her hand in marriage. Mr Lambert was unimpressed.

He was even less impressed the following day after he had met the young gentleman. No man is ever good enough for a father but this one seemed a shifty, spineless sort of fellow that Mr Lambert had no intention of allowing to marry his daughter, whatever his title.

Sir Henry had foreseen such a strategy. He was used to being found wanting by prospective fathers-in-law. On their next clandestine meeting he comforted Sarah and told her that there were other ways of skinning a cat.

Poor Mr Lambert had organised a ball to try to distract Sarah. He had not thought of it before but now it seemed a good idea to let Sarah have something else than idiots to think about. It all seemed to go very well, most of the best families of east Herefordshire came but, towards the end of the evening, he realised that he had not seen his daughter for some time. A search was made but all that was found was a satin slipper on the drive.

Sarah was already bitterly regretting her decision to elope. Sir Henry had told her that he would send a coach to meet her at the bottom of a nearby road called Chance's

Pitch, but there had been no sign of it. It was January, it was cold and pouring with rain. For three hours she wandered in the dark and wet, feeling that her world had come to an end. Then the coachman found her, at Barton Holloway. He had gone to the wrong place, Blackmore Pitch. As Sir Henry comforted her and cursed the coachman she started to feel that this was just one small initial problem and her life was now straightforward.

They married in a far-off church on special licence and then returned to Hope End. Sir Henry came armed with a lawyer and declared that he was the true owner of the house. He had been careful in his research and had discovered that Sarah's mother had left the house directly to Sarah so Sarah's husband had better title than Mr Lambert. Her father was evicted and forced to go to live in his second-best house at nearby Barton Court. Sir Henry told his worried wife that the marriage could never be a happy one with old misery glowering at them all day.

Even so, the marriage did not turn into a happy one. Sir Henry, now he was master of Hope End, seemed to find many faults with his wife. It was not long before she too was evicted from the house. She tried to see her father but he would not let her into his presence, so angry was he with his loss that she had engineered. She went to live with a poor relative but her heart was broken and she did not stay long in this world that had let her down so badly.

Then the stories started. People started avoiding Barton Holloway, a narrow, sunken road, after dark. They started saying it was haunted and they were in no doubt what lurked there, the ghost of a young woman in a dark gown. To see it is to be overcome with a feeling of unutterable sadness and no young woman would ever walk down that lane for many years after, for fear of seeing the ghost and bringing ill luck to her marriage prospects.

A man cannot escape his past and it was not long before Sir Henry Tempest had run through another fortune and was forced to sell Hope End to a slave owner named Barrett.

The Barretts were, by all accounts, a happy family. But things did not go well for them at Hope End. One of the daughters, Elizabeth, had a riding accident near Barton Holloway and was an invalid for the rest of her life. Edward Barrett's wife died and then came slave emancipation. Despite handsome remuneration, he too had to sell Hope End and retire to the town house in Wimpole Street.

Elizabeth Barrett must have known about the unhappy ghost of Barton Holloway but that did not prevent her conducting her own elopement, with her fellow poet Robert Browning. Fortunately that marriage seems to have been a happy one.

THE GHOST
OF HEREFORD
CATHEDRAL

Mr Hoskins had always worked in the cathedral. At least, that is what it felt to the other staff, clergy and those people of Hereford who had anything to do with the building. The longest-serving canon, the other sacristans and the eldest member of the congregation could all remember, when they first came to the cathedral, having Mr Hoskins pointed out to them as already an ancient fixture in the place.

No one knew his Christian name. He was always referred to as Mr Hoskins and no one, not even the Dean, would have been so bold as to ask such a private gentleman what his name was. His duties were to prepare the building for all divine offices and to tidy up afterwards. Not too onerous a job and one, in earlier years, that he had performed with exemplary efficiency. But, by 1785, he was getting older and people were noticing that he was becoming infirm in both mind and body.

What used to take him a brisk half hour was now taking him a stiff hour and a quarter, which caused problems. He seemed completely unaware of the changes that were happening to him and started his preparations at his usual time, which meant that, when services were due to start, he was still fussing about the nave. Given his seniority within the confines of the cathedral precinct he would bicker with junior clergy when they were sent to chide him and hurry him up. The last straw came when the bishop, sitting on his throne during a Sunday matins, found no Book of Common Prayer in its accustomed place. He was forced to share with his chaplain, his face red with the indignity of it.

What he said to the Dean after the service was not recorded. It was a private meeting and the Dean certainly never said anything about it afterwards. But the Dean did seek out Mr Hoskins the following day while the latter was dusting the lectern eagle.

"My dear Mr Hoskins," the Dean opened. This stopped Mr Hoskins in mid brush. It was a long time since the Dean had last spoken to him.

"I fear we have been a little bit remiss. You have been a good and faithful servant to this building but tempus fugit, as the poet says."

Mr Hoskins said nothing but the occasional flick of his brush on the brass of the eagle seemed to signify assent. He had no idea what tempus fugit meant but assumed it was something religious.

The Dean gazed at the West window as if looking for divine inspiration. "So perhaps we have been a little unfair to you. We should have discussed a proper pension before now."

Mr Hoskins stopped his brushing. "I ain't leaving."

"Do not fear Mr Hoskins. We will see that the pension is more than adequate for your means."

"I ain't leaving."

Thinking that he had done all that could be expected of him and not wanting a confrontation in the cathedral, the Dean turned on his heels and returned to the Deanery. He saw to it that the financial matters were settled as he had promised and he himself wrote a glowing testimonial that praised Mr Hoskins's work but also set a date after which his services would no longer be required.

When this was delivered to Mr Hoskins he spent a good passage of time deciphering it and then, when its import had fully been realised, he ripped it into small pieces.

The appointed day arrived but Mr Hoskins turned up as usual and carried on about his duties as if nothing was different. The Dean broke a sherry glass when he heard about it. The next day two vergers were set to guard the North Door and to prevent Mr Hoskins's entrance when he arrived. Still he tried to elbow his way between them like a man possessed, but to no avail.

Then he was seen in Hereford no longer. After three days word came to the cathedral that Mr Hoskins had been found dead at his lodgings in West Street. Some people thought it must have been just old age and some people said it was a broken heart.

His funeral service was held in the cathedral. Where else could it have been? While the Dean could not attend, a senior canon officiated. There was no question of him being actually buried within the cathedral, he did not warrant that, but still most felt that he had been treated well.

A few days later Canon Underwood was walking along the Great Crossing on his way to the Vicars Choral. As was usual he glanced towards the High Altar as he passed it and saw the familiar figure of Mr Hoskins cleaning the misericords in the Choir. He walked on and was almost out of the building when he pulled up with a start. Hoskins was dead. The hairs on the back of his neck rose and he shivered.

Nervously he retraced his steps and looked into the Choir. It was empty. He must have imagined it. He carried on thankfully about his business but more shaken than he wanted to be.

But over the next few days people less concerned about their personal dignity started telling their friends that they too had seen old Hoskins. Soon the news spread all over Hereford that Hoskins's ghost walked in the cathedral. Inevitably the crowds came flocking. If the Dean thought that Hoskins had been a nuisance to him in life he found that the old man had become a greater curse to him in death.

All thoughts of sanctity and silence were forgotten. It was almost impossible to conduct evensong without being interrupted by a terrible mixture of the better off, putting their theories of the Enlightenment to the test, and the lower orders, come to gawp.

The Dean and Chapter met, with the sole item on the agenda that something must be done. In the end twelve parsons were assembled. They trooped into the cathedral at eleven o'clock one night, each carrying a candle, a Bible and a prayer book. They drew a chalk circle all around them, for protection. In the middle was a table. On this they placed the twelve candles, twelve Bibles and twelve prayer books. They sat without speaking until twelve o'clock. While the clock was striking they each lit their candle and called the ghost. After a great deal of praying it came and pretty angry it was by all accounts, but it could not resist twelve clergyman and they managed to confine it into a silver snuff-box. They all knew it must be laid under running water, so Canon Underwood ran as fast as his arthritic legs could carry him to Bysters Gate, the old medieval entrance to the east of the city, and dropped the box over the bridge into the brook. When the Canon eventually made it home that night his shirt was ringing wet; at least according to his servant-girl and she ought to know.

Were their efforts successful? Certainly there were no reports of sightings in the cathedral after this point so they must have been congratulating themselves on a job well done when the West Tower of the cathedral collapsed, taking with it the spire of the East Tower. The cathedral was in ruins for several years and some people saw this as old Hoskins's revenge. When the West Front was eventually re-built those same people saw the replacement as old Hoskins's continuing revenge. So unpopular was it that, by popular acclamation, it had to be re-done in 1902, although many people thought the result was not much better.

Byster's Gate has gone now. The workmen who took it down were heard to remark that they hoped they would not disturb old Hoskins.

Perhaps they did because some people, coming out of the Kerry Arms pub, which stands on the spot, have reported being passed by an old man dressed in black and a shiver has gone down their spines. If it happens to you, do not worry. It is only old Hoskins going about his business.

THE TWO MISS DAVIES

Dorothea and Doris Davies lived on a farm near Bromyard. They had lived there from time immemorial so that, when they died within a couple of days of each other, it seemed a great change to the local people.

The sad fact was that they had run a once-prosperous farm into the ground. Their father had been a man noted for taking advantage of every new technique that he could find out about and at that time, at the end of the eighteenth century, there were a lot of innovations to find out about. His daughters were totally different and would not allow any change. Everything must be done the way their father had done it. Whereas he had been a good employer, they were a cantankerous old pair and no one would stay there long.

It was a wonder to many that they were able to pay the rent but the place was little better than a rural slum and, after their death, no one could be found to take on the tenancy. These were difficult times for farmers but, of course, if you listen to them, there has never been any other time.

Eventually, a new tenant was found, one who came from far away and did not know the farm's recent history.

Now people are terrible at making up stories. Before long the indoor servants were talking about the strange clattering and banging that shook the house every night to anyone who would listen. So it was not long before no servant or labourer was prepared to stay in the farmhouse overnight. They preferred to find lodgings in other, quieter, houses and come to their work well after dawn.

This did not please the farmer. He wanted someone who would light the kitchen fire and cook his breakfast and he was not too happy that his men were wasting good working time walking to the farm from wherever they lodged.

The farmer's need for an indoor servant spread far and wide but no one locally could be found willing to take on the work.

One day there was a knock on the door and when the farmer opened it there was a little slip of a thing standing there.

"Good day to you Mr Turvey. I'm Mary Price from Hereford and I've come to help you out."

Now Ernest Turvey did not much care for impertinence and there was something about this girl that seemed to say there was quite a bit of impertinence in her. But farmers in need of a good cooked breakfast cannot be choosers and he decided to give her a go.

"Since you're not from these parts, it's only fair to tell you that there is some silly talk about this place, noises in the night and other tomfoolery. Will that worry you?"

"Good Lord sir, I've come across much worse things in Hereford. I'm not afraid of the Devil hisself."

Taking that as a positive advantage for the job, the farmer agreed to hire her.

That very evening, Mary was dozing in the kitchen chair. She had prepared the master a good supper and he had gone to bed happier than he had for a long time. She had not been dozing for long when a terrible clattering and banging started up. She looked around but the kitchen was completely empty. Even though she was now fully awake the noise carried on and any normal person would have been out of the door and running as fast as they could.

But not Mary. Instead she looked around the empty kitchen.

"I'm not afraid of you," she said. "In the name of God who are you?" which is the correct way with ghosts, though how she knew that is another story.

There was a movement in the corner of her eye and, when she turned to look, there were two old ladies, dressed in a peculiar fashion and smiling at her in what Mary thought was not a malicious way but more one of relief. They started to beckon to her and Mary, without bothering to think too clearly about the situation, got up off her chair and followed them.

They set off down the cellar steps and Mary, taking her candle with her, came down behind them. They seemed to glide down whereas Mary was hard put to it to keep her balance, there being no handrail. By the time she got to the bottom the two spectres were in the middle of the cellar, pointing urgently at a particular flagstone. Miming that she was just popping back upstairs, Mary went and fetched an old shovel that was out the back, that the farmer used to scrape mud and muck off the yard.

When she returned the two old ladies were still there, though possibly a bit more agitated. Mary shooed them away from the flagstone and struck the shovel as hard as she could into a crack beside it. She carried on with this work, the two ethereal spinsters hanging onto each other, jiggling up and down in excitement until she had enough leverage to force the flagstone out of its ancient setting. It clumped over onto its other side, revealing a dark hole. By now the two apparitions were almost dancing up and down and gesticulating madly at the hole.

Mary reached down and pulled out an old leather bag and showed it to the ghosts. They gave her a look of joy and thankfulness and then completely disappeared.

When the farmer got up the next morning he was annoyed that the fires were not lit and there was no sound of his breakfast being prepared, but when he saw what was lying on the kitchen table all thoughts of breakfast went out of his mind. There was a pile of gold coins and a note in his servant's ragged handwriting. "This is half. I found it so I'm taking half. It's your ground so you can have the other."

What became of Mary he never could discover, but he hoped she had made a good path for her life. He did not begrudge her the gold that she had taken. He was particularly happy that no more strange noises and moanings were ever heard on his farm again.

HETTY WALWYN

Hetty had always been a pretty child. On the occasions that she was seen around the village of Much Marcle the old women would shake their heads and say, "Mark my words. She'll break some young man's heart one day." They did not know how right they would be.

It was the best life the eighteenth century had to offer. Her father was the owner of Hellens, which he considered by far the finest mansion in the county. He was not an overly ambitious man and he had a good supply of both sons and daughters, so she might avoid the worst fate of girls in a rich house, that she would be used as a pawn in some marriage game of aggrandisement. But perhaps there are even worse fates.

Hers was a life of enjoyment and accomplishments. From an early age, the one she took most delight in was riding. Although forced to ride side-saddle, she was still determined to do everything that a boy of her age would be expected to do. She loved her home but also she loved the taste of freedom that riding gave her. By the time she was eighteen she could outdistance any of the chaperones that her father sent with her and was riding on her own over the south east of the county.

Although Herefordshire was a reasonably quiet place, still her father worried. In the end, he decided to send one of the grooms, a son of one of his farming tenants and of good character, off with her to make sure she came to no harm. He, at least, could keep up with her.

So it went through the months of a long and warm

summer. If people had looked closely they might have seen that Hetty came back now with an extra glow in her cheeks, that she was laughing more than she used to and, on wet days when there could be no riding, took to gazing out of the window in the direction of the stables and generally making life difficult for the servants. Young Bill Williams came in for terrible ribbing from his fellow grooms, who could see how the land was lying better than the Walwyns, but he was a gentlemanly soul and would not discuss the subject.

In the autumn the weather inevitably became wetter and there were fewer days when Hetty could go riding. One day when it was clear the two went out and were later coming back than usual. In the household there were fears, thought, not yet spoken, that some misfortune had taken place.

At last they were seen coming back along the long drive but it was clear there was something amiss. Hetty was on Bill's horse and Bill was leading Hetty's which was badly lame. Nearer still and Hetty could be seen to be covered in mud. This led to a flutter of horror among the female servants that brought the master out to see what all the fuss was about.

"What happened to you Hetty?"

"I fell and my horse went lame."

"Are you hurt?"

"No."

Seeing the matter settled, Mr Walwyn went back inside. Bill took both horses back to the stables and a hot bath was prepared for Hetty. There the matter should have ended but the women who knew her found Hetty much more subdued than she normally was after a ride. In the grooms' quarters Bill was also strangely quiet and it did not take long for his fellows to wheedle out what was the matter with him given how much it was praying on his mind. Hetty's fall had not been a ladylike slip from the saddle. It was a full "arse over tit", as they called it in the stable, during which, in those days before knickers, Bill had seen more than he thought he should.

Bill feared for his place but Hetty said nothing. For a countryman like Mr Walwyn, a fall off a horse was nothing out of the ordinary. In fact, he insisted that she go out riding again the following day, although she complained that she was still too stiff from her fall. As Bill brought the horses around to the front an observant person might have been surprised at how much they both blushed and how quiet they were as they trotted off together. However, that same person might have noticed how freely they were laughing together when they returned and that, on subsequent mornings, a new relationship seemed to have developed between them.

It was just before Christmas that a very nervous groom came in through the servant's entrance and asked to see his master. That half-an-hour waiting must have been the worst of his life. When he was eventually allowed in to see Mr Walwyn, the meeting did not last long. There was a bellow of rage and then the unfortunate Williams came flying out of the room. White-faced he went straight to his quarters and started packing his few belongings.

Mr Walwyn sent immediately for Hetty and there

was another scene. After some more bellowing, this time replied to in wails, she too went to her room and stayed there for two days, no sustenance being brought her.

Without Bill Williams around and Hetty not wanting to go riding again, things seemed to quieten down and Mr Walwyn congratulated himself on a storm ridden out.

On Christmas Day itself Hetty was late coming down to breakfast. This irritated her father, who liked to keep to tradition and the tradition was that they should all breakfast together on this day before attending church. He sent a maid to her bedroom who, a few minutes later, came running back to say that the bed had not been slept in. A search was undertaken and, when it reached the Williams' farm, Bill was also found to be missing. It was all Mr Walwyn could do not to turn the family out on the spot but their obvious distress at the disgrace that their son had brought upon them softened his heart.

Nothing was heard from the eloping couple and five years went by. Then a bedraggled figure came trudging along the drive towards the house. There was something familiar about her. The eldest sister realised first it was Hetty. Though Mr Walwyn would not see her, she was taken into the drawing room, given tea and bread and her story listened to.

She and Bill had been married in Bristol and then taken a ship to the American colonies. There Bill had prospered as a merchant and built up a good trade in sugar and tea. She saw her siblings snigger at this unlikely story and pulled her right hand free of her ragged cloak to expose a bright diamond ring that she said Bill had given her to mark their prosperity. But a fever had come to the colony. Bill caught it and died. Hetty had tried to keep the business going but, with no training, had been repeatedly cheated until she was forced to sell up and barely had enough to buy passage back to England and return to her native country. The only thing she had left of their life together was the diamond ring.

Mr Walwyn was not a hard man. He would have been completely within his rights to put her out of doors. But he let her remain. He let her have her old bedroom back. The only condition was that she was never to leave that room. She must stay there, day and night, so that no more temptation would be put before her. The windows were barred and her only communication with the outside world was a bell rope that rang a bell on the roof when she needed anything.

That bell tolling, reminding the world of the house's shame, and the white face looking out on a world that once held so much excitement, became a constant feature of the house.

In a few years Mr Walwyn died and his eldest son came back from London to manage the estate. This brought some freeing of Hetty's restrictions. Her sisters were now allowed to occasionally visit her.

A few years after that and Hetty herself died. Did Hetty regret the turns her life had taken? After her death her relatives found, scratched on the window with a diamond ring, these words:

> It is a virtue to abstain
> From what we love
> If it prove our bane.

But some of the servants said they still saw her white face looking down at them from her window and there was something about her old room; none of them could be got to go in there on their own. Even though the bell had long been disconnected it could still be occasionally heard ringing.

In the Second World War, a young officer staying in the house came down to breakfast one morning complaining of being woken up in the middle of the night by an old woman in a dressing gown. He was assured that there was no one of that description staying in the house. Then it was recalled that he had been given Hetty's old room to sleep in the previous night.

HIGGINS'S WELL

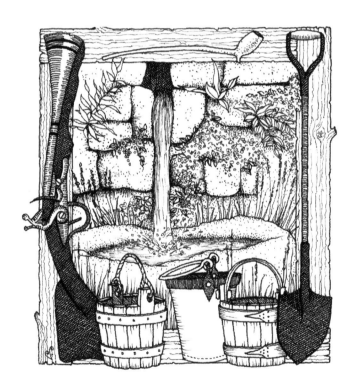

The life of a farmer is a hard one. Do not believe anyone who tells you anything to the contrary. It is one reason why they are so miserable all the time.

Such was "Old Higgins" who farmed down by Little Birch almost three hundred years ago. In some way he had cause to be miserable. It was hilly country and the sun took a long time to warm his fields in the spring and did not bother to warm them at all in the winter so that the frost stayed late into the morning like a bad guest. The frost was his only guest because he was so miserable that he lived alone and did not take kindly to visitors; the sort of man for whom the word cantankerous was invented.

But equally he had little reason to be so miserable. At least he had land, which was more than most people in the country could boast. The land was good enough to feed himself and pay the rent. He was a good and devious hunter and so ate meat on a regular basis.

If you had the misfortune to meet him and somehow managed to get him talking he would only tell you about the bad things. He genuinely did not contemplate the good things. To him counting your blessings would seem a very odd practice.

All that was wrong with his life was centred on the spring on his land. These were the days long before most people had good clean water piped directly into their homes. Those times are not that far off; my own father remembered the time when he got a belt for fetching the nearby pond water rather than going down to the stream to bringing back fresh running water for the cider making.

In those days people appreciated good water and could tell the difference from one source to another. As luck would have it, the spring on Higgins's land was particularly pure and sweet. So, although people might have had a nearer choice, there was an almost constant stream of people and their animals to Higgins's spring to get at the good water.

Old Higgins could not abide such a thing. It seemed almost every time he looked out of his window there would be one neighbour or another trespassing on his land with a bucket. Soon it became known that, if you wanted to drink the sweet water, you would have to risk the rough tongue of Old Higgins or worse, because he kept an old, rusty blunderbuss by the door.

That only made things worse because the villagers now came at dawn and dusk. There was barely a morning when Old Higgins was not woken up by the clank of buckets or an evening when he did not lie in his bed shaking with anger at the sound of a couple of his neighbours greeting each other merrily as they extracted water from his spring.

Being a resourceful man he decided to do something about it. One day he loaded up his cart with stones. He went down to the spring and started blocking it up. When all the stones were in place he got his spade and covered them with earth. It took him all of that day but he had the satisfaction, just as he was patting the last earth down, to see young Billy Toase walking up towards him.

"You might as well turn around and go back the way

you came. There'll be no water for you here today or ever again."

Billy came up and looked at the spring dumbfounded. His were not the quickest of wits and it was taking a bit of time to realise the great change that had happened on the hillside.

"You filled her in maister?"

"I have indeed."

"You've done a terrible thing there."

"Bad for you, good for me. Now get back and tell them there will be no more water at my expense."

Higgins watched Billy's slumped shoulders as the young man retreated down the hill, the empty bucket jangling disconsolately. He grinned more than he had in the last ten years.

He was still grinning that evening as he sat by his fireside. His back and arms were aching with the effort of the day but his heart was almost singing with his cleverness. He filled a clay pipe with tobacco and was looking forward to a quiet smoke when he suddenly realised that there was a figure standing in his doorway. It made him jump. He was not used to visitors.

When his eyes became accustomed to looking at the light he saw it was old Barbara Barrett. Of all the figures it could have been this was the one that Higgins wanted to see the least, because Barbara had a reputation for her tongue that rivalled his and it was generally considered in the locality that she knew rather more than she should do about the workings of plants and what they could do for you.

"You've done a bad thing maister."

"I'm having a quiet smoke in my kitchen for the first time in I don't know how long. It seems a good thing to me."

"The Lady will not like it."

"What lady? This is Stanhope land. No lady has any say in it."

"That is what you think, but you might not think it for very much longer."

Probably Old Higgins blinked at the wrong moment, but when he looked again the old woman was gone. Higgins shivered a bit but then lit his pipe and thought no more about it.

Whoever spread it, whether Barbara had a hand in it or people actually saw something mysterious, the rumours began to grow that the guardian of the spring was angry and there was going to be trouble. At market day in Hereford, Higgins had never been popular but now he felt as if people were actually going out of their way to shun him. He did what any Hereford man would do in the circumstances. He told them they could go to blazes and thought he was better off without them.

He was sitting in his kitchen smoking his pipe and with a self-satisfied smile on his face thinking about how annoyed the villagers were with him when he realised that his feet were cold. He shook them and they splashed instead of knocking on the hard kitchen floor.

He looked down and saw that the floor was covered by several inches of water. For a sickening moment he thought his house was sinking but then he pulled himself together. It just must be some form of flood.

He stood up and waded along the floor to the door. By that time the water had pushed up the flagstones by the chimney and was welling up with the force of a fountain. In something of a panic he rushed out into the dusk. Automatically he looked down his fields to the spring. A white figure was standing there and a cold fear ran down his spine. It seemed to Higgins that the thing was staring at him reproachfully. It was too far away to see its eyes, thank God, but he still seemed to feel them burning into him.

He staggered and almost fell back into the flood in his kitchen, desperately clutching his door jamb to save himself.

When he looked again the figure was gone. He rushed to his shed and fetched a spade. Down to the spring he went, with some trepidation. Within half an hour the work of a few days ago was undone and the spring flowed freely again.

When he came back to his kitchen the fountain had stopped although the floor was still awash.

It would be nice to say that, after this incident, Old Higgins was a changed person, full of love for his fellow man. That was not the case. Within a few days of trespassers resuming their trek onto his land he had made a field drain from the spring down to the road so that people could collect the water without going onto his land. Still, it seemed to work because the people of Little Birch got their water and Higgins saw no more figures in white down by his spring. And, if you take a walk from Much Birch to Little Birch, as you walk along a pleasant lane you will come across the neat culvert in the side of the hill that is still called Higgins's Well.

Now you are sensible people and know that it was all caused by the pressure of the blocked spring welling back. While it is still light outside I will agree with you. However the fact remains that, where there is a public amenity that people have valued for generations, you are a fool to mess with it.

THE SIN-EATER

No one chooses to become a sin-eater. The taking unto oneself the sins of others is a dangerous and squalid business. Only the very poorest and degraded will take on the risk of eternal damnation in return for sixpence, a loaf of bread and a bowl of beer.

But such a man was Jack Clement, a long, lean, ugly, lamentable poor rascal who lived in a tiny hovel just outside Ross, on the road to Monmouth. He was known locally as "the Scrape", because he scraped his existence from one day to the next and had started out, like his father before him, as a landless labourer but did not really apply himself even to this, preferring the temptations of drink and moaning about his lot in taverns, so that, when his physical strength began to wane, no farmer cared enough about him to find him odd jobs about the place and his family saw no advantage in helping him out, however much he might suggest the idea.

When one of his tavern cronies had tried to do something by suggesting he become a sin-eater, it was not necessarily malicious advice. Jasper had come across him in their usual Ross ale-house bemoaning his lot and how he did not even have enough coin to buy his own beer. Jasper had heard the previous day that they were looking for a sin-eater over Orcop way. Naturally and helpfully he gave his opinion that such a thing was a convenient way of earning a bowl of beer and money to buy more.

Jack had a vague idea of what a sin-eater was. He had occasionally seen one at funerals that he had attended but had not taken much note of them, being more interested in the free beer that was usually available. He knew that, in return for the bread, beer and money, the sin-eater took on the sins of the deceased, so to ease their passage into heaven. Complacently he reasoned that he had accrued more than enough sins upon himself already and a few more would make little difference. So he walked to Orcop, offered his services and was taken on, no questions asked.

When the coffin was brought out of the old man's cottage and laid on the bier, Jack took a step backwards. He had never played a prominent part in a funeral before and the prospect was suddenly unappealing. But there was a great press of people behind him and his options were limited. He felt a push that sent him towards the bier, close to the coffin. Opposite him the deceased's eldest son gave him a look of disgust and then handed him a loaf of bread across the coffin. Jack immediately forgot the look, he was only concentrating on the bread. It was a good-sized loaf of white flour. He could barely stop himself drooling onto the coffin. Then he was given the maple bowl brimming with beer. Out of delicacy he put the bread on the ground and took it with both hands so as not to drop beer onto the coffin. It smelt as if it was a good drop. Finally he was handed a small bag that clinked agreeably.

"We have given you food, drink and money. Do you now take on my father's sins?" asked the man, in a slightly accusing voice.

"I do," replied Jack, in his best voice, that he used for magistrates when he came up before them. Then the cortege moved on to keep its appointment with the grave and he was left with his winnings. Taking a sip of the beer, Jack thought that he must have the best job in the country.

Slowly news got around the county that here was a sin-eater who, if not exactly respectable, at least would not cause disgrace at their relative's funeral. Jobs started to trickle in. Jack started to hope for a harsh winter.

Then Captain Robert Croft died. As his name suggested, he was a member of the illustrious Croft family, but a cadet branch, just enough money to keep up the appearance of a gentleman and just enough noble blood to raise hell. After an inauspicious military career during which he spilt more English blood than that of the enemy through duels over women and gambling debts, he retired to the Herefordshire countryside, to cause mayhem amongst the local foxes and maidens. If he ever knew how close he often came to death from his daredevil riding over high Herefordshire hedges or outraged fathers he made no show of it. Eventually it was the port that took him, having taken the warning signs that his body could take no more with the disdain he had treated everything else in his life, including his wife. That unfortunate woman, a once beautiful, once rich heiress from Brecon, still, amazingly, held some affection for her late and widely-unlamented husband. But she was not blind to his faults. That is why she called for a sin-eater.

A horseman arrived outside the Scrapes's hovel. He did not normally receive visitors who rode, nor did they knock loudly on his door with a riding crop. He was disinclined to open the door, but another knock broke a panel in the rotten door and he was staring at a man dressed in black who glowered at him through the gap.

"You are the sin-eater?"

Jack confessed that he was. "Captain Croft will be buried at midday at Bodenham church. Be there."

With that he got back on his horse, turned it around and was away. Jack spent the rest of the day pacing his small room. He had heard of Captain Croft's reputation. Certainly there was someone who needed to off-load as many sins as he could before he met his maker. But previously Jack had only taken onto himself such peccadilloes as the poor were able to afford. Taking on the sins of the gentry seemed a higher order of risk. On the other hand he had almost a superstitious dread of upsetting his betters. He knew no good would come from that either.

Of course he went but regretted it as soon as he got there, feeling his fellow mourners move away from him with even greater rapidity than they normally did. The wind had got up and it was overcast. Although it was only August there was already an autumnal bite to the air. He did not know where to stand to be inconspicuous.

Suddenly there was a new tension in the air as the hearse arrived. It was a magnificent sight. Four black horses, each with a black plume of feathers on its head, the hearse, glazed like a coach, the coffin, draped in the Union flag. When the coffin was dragged out of the hearse and placed on the common parish bier, Captain Croft was a mortal like anyone else, one of the undertakers pointed at Jack and beckoned him over. The crowd parted like the Red Sea and he found his legs taking him towards the coffin.

No relative but a paid undertaker stood across from him. He almost threw the loaf, which Jack was disappointed to see was a poor, brown variety, and came close to slopping the beer onto the coffin, such was his clear distaste for the farce he was being made to go through. But Jack's mood changed when he saw the money. Not a bag of pence but an honest-to-goodness gold sovereign was handed to him.

"Do you take on the sins?" sneered the undertaker. Jack said that he did, but his mind was on the bright gold coin that he was holding, he could not think of anything else. When he reached out to take it he felt a dull but terrible pain in his back, as if someone had stabbed him. He cried out and looked accusingly behind him but there was no one standing within knife distance. He barely noticed the coffin and the crowd moving into the church, only that he was suddenly alone. Eagerly clutching the coin he made his way home.

When he was safely back, the first thing he did was hide the coin in the rotten thatch of his roof. There, he reasoned, no one would have cause or wish to look for it. He laughed to himself at the prize, so easy got. His thoughts turned to how he could get more.

Before that moment Jack had always been a person who kept himself to himself. If someone wanted to buy him a drink that was fine by him, but otherwise he preferred his own company. Now people found that they could not get away from the fellow. Whichever pub they went into in Ross he seemed to be in it. Not sitting quietly and morosely by himself but sidling up to you, laughing at the look of distaste on your face. What was wrong with the fool? Now he always seemed to be asking questions and they always seemed to be questions about money. Some people put it down to the fact that, after his appearance at Captain Croft's funeral, he saw himself as sin-eater to the gentry. It had gone to his head.

But Jack Clement was hunting and, after a few days, he had found his quarry. Thomas Walsh was a moderately successful butcher in the town. Unlike most butchers he was quiet and withdrawn, not the fat, jolly soul people expected for someone in close proximity to all that meat. That led to talk, that he had squirrelled away a fortune somewhere in his shop, that was why he never mixed with his fellow tradesmen.

Thomas Walsh had gone to bed at his usual time. Tomorrow would be killing day. He could hear the beasts he had bought at market lowing in the pound at the back of the shop. He never slept soundly on such nights. He was therefore still awake when he thought he heard a scraping noise outside. God knows what miscreants are about in Ross at night, but he had a good strong door. He turned over in his feather bed and tried to get some sleep.

Then the scraping came from outside his own bedroom door. He sat bolt upright. "Who's there?" No answer, but it was not quite silence. He could have sworn he could hear someone breathing on the other side of the door. Thomas Walsh jumped out of bed, grabbed the cleaver that he kept handy and went to open the door.

The magistrate who was given the task of investigating the crime always said that he never saw a thing like it. First of all there was the blood, more than you would think was possible to come out of a man's body. Then there was the spectacle of a respectable butcher gutted as if he was one of his own beasts. Then it was the marks all over the walls, as if some giant animal had tried to claw through them. If Thomas Walsh really did have a hoard of coin, it was never found.

There was no finer tailor than Neville Lingen. The gentry came from as far away as Hereford to be fitted by him. It was therefore common knowledge that he must have a tidy sum put away. A few nights after Walsh's death he was found in a back alley, bleeding profusely from a hundred little wounds, almost pinpricks, incoherent, talking about wolves. He died before sunrise.

Tradespeople have to make a living however they can, and violent death is never good for the soul, so in both instances, the sin-eater was employed to free the likely burden on the two men. People who had not seen Clement for some time were shocked by his appearance. They had not expected it could get any worse but it had. His hair, under his greasy hat, had grown long and tangled, his clothes were even more ragged and his fingernails, some were long and sharp, others had been torn off. But his smile, as if he was thinking of a secret known only to himself, was the thing that worried them the most.

Old Sydney Powell always liked to tell anyone who would listen that his family had once been rich but had lost all their money supporting the king in the Great Rebellion. God knows it might even have been true, there were enough of such people about. Now he did odd jobs around the town, was no trouble to anyone and was fondly regarded by all the townsfolk as a local landmark. When he was found with his throat torn out, lying in the churchyard, there was general annoyance, enough was enough.

For some reason, suspicion fell on the most despised, Jack Clement. Men of sensibility said this was all superstition and would do nothing, but a few lads, up for some community action, took some Dutch courage at various hostelries and, when it was nice and dark, set off to see Jack to find out what he knew about the matter.

A hovel can be as forbidding as a castle if you are in the right frame of mind. It had been all right when they were walking along Wilton Bridge but now that they had turned the corner and the sin-eater's home stood out like a black stain in a black night, their minds cleared and turning around started to appear a good option. They might have done too if Jack Clement had not that moment chosen to come out of the door and stare at them. The few who talked about it afterwards said that his eyes shone red and he hissed at them like a cat. They also alleged that he came for them rather than them going for him. A charge will always gain some momentary advantage but there were five of them, even if the one fought like one possessed. Despite suffering scratches and bites they got him onto the ground. Then there was a momentary hiatus because nobody knew what to do next. But Billy Price hated ambiguity. He picked up a large stone lying by the side of the road and brought it down on Jack Clement's head.

"Christ, Billy, what have you done?"

"What we came to do."

After that there was no choice. By unexpressed consent they carried the body and dropped it over Wilton Bridge, satisfied by the sound of the body hitting the water. Then they went home, letting the drink dissipate and the fear of the hangman's noose grow.

Some people thought the disappearance another victim claimed by the demon. Then, when there were no more deaths, people started putting two and two together. No one came forward to take the sin-eater's place and people had to go to purgatory and suffer for their own sins.

OLD MAID'S WALK

Gardens were invented in the seventeenth century. Yes, before that people had vegetable patches and herb plots but it was only when plant hunters went out to the Middle East, China and the Americas and brought back gaudy blooms that flower gardens really took off. But such plants were obviously going to be very expensive so it was only the aristocrats and the gentry who were able to indulge in this hobby.

Such a one was Charles Markey, the owner of Alton Court, just outside Ross-on-Wye. He had become obsessed by his garden and was determined it would become the most beautiful in the county. As he walked in it he had dreams of all the rich and important people he would be able to persuade to visit it. His garden was the vehicle by which his family would rise to new heights.

Of course Mr Markey did not do the gardening himself. He employed some local labourers and an expensive head gardener who was supposed to know his stuff but, when an unexpected late frost killed off most of his most cherished specimens, Mr Markey flew into the temper for which he was well known in the area and dismissed the head gardener out of hand.

He set out to find a replacement but that was not an easy task, all the good ones were taken and Mr Markey was nervous of poaching someone from a great household. The expense, for one thing, would be prohibitive. The only person who remotely fitted the bill was a young fellow called Ralph Mortimer. Mr Markey, like most people of the elder generation, set great store by age and experience, but, forced to give the young man a trial, he was surprised by just how knowledgeable the young fellow was. Under his care Alton Court's garden flourished as never before and Mr Markey could see his plans being realised.

There was one other thing Mr Markey held against young Mortimer. He knew for a fact that Ralph's mother was a poor widow woman from Ullingswick and, outside his salary, Ralph did not have a penny to his name. Yet he would tell anyone who was stupid enough to listen that he was descended from the great Mortimers of Wigmore Castle. Charles put no store by a pedigree that stretched back to the Dark Ages; money, and the power it gave you, that was all that mattered.

What Mr Markey did not notice, and it might have given him more pause for thought if he had, was that Ralph was immensely good looking, a fact that had not escaped the attention of the kitchen maids, who were all of a twitter from the first day of him working there. It also did not escape the attention of Clara, Markey's second daughter, herself a noted beauty. She had always enjoyed a walk in her father's garden, in early morning or at sunset, when the sun's rays were not too bright. Now her walks became even more frequent. If anyone noticed it the news did not reach the ears of Mr Markey.

Soon the two young people were exchanging gardening lore. Ralph might have saved a particularly fine bloom to hand her, Clara might have purloined a sweetmeat from the cook. On such exchanges their hands might momentarily touch.

Given her father's predisposition Clara and Ralph knew better than to make their romance public. They snatched what moments together that they could. If anyone else was in the garden when Clara took her walks they remained aloof, apart from furtive glances. It was only when they were alone that they could gaze into each other's eyes and express their undying love for each other.

If Mr Markey had an inkling of his daughter's affection he made no show of it. His next actions might be purely down to his dynastic ambitions. He entered into negotiations with the Rudhalls, the most powerful family in Ross, for one of their younger sons to marry Clara. When he sat his daughter down and explained how successful his negotiations had been he no doubt expected her to be overjoyed, so often are fathers deceived by their own hearts thinking they speak for their daughter's. Instead, she let out a terrible cry that froze him to the marrow and burst into inexplicable tears. His only option was to attribute it to an excess of female humours.

In a short time a similar depression could be seen in Ralph, though he would not tell his friends what the problem might be. Clara's hysteria did not abate and the servants of Alton Court made their own assumptions. Here was a young woman who should be at the height of happiness. That she was not could only be put down to witchcraft. Near the Court lived an old woman called Nancy Cartwright. It became a generally understood thing that she must be behind Clara's mood. Out of the goodness of their hearts they made crosses out of straw and flung them in front of the old woman. When that did not work they grabbed hold of her and prodded her with pins in the attempt to break the spell but nothing could shake Clara's despond.

The day of the wedding marched ever nearer and the secret meetings between the two lovers became increasingly more desperate. One morning a couple of boys were leaning over Wilton Bridge, hoping to catch sight of some salmon, when they saw a man's hat stuck against the central pillar. When they made their discovery known people feared the worst and a search was undertaken. Sure enough, upstream near the field known as the Acres, a body was discovered. When it was dragged out of the water it was immediately identified as young Ralph Mortimer.

The body was taken to the Welsh Harp Inn in Alton Street, where an inquest was held. There were no marks of violence on the body and his friends testified to Ralph's lack of spirits over the last few weeks. There was no other outcome possible. The jury decided that Ralph Mortimer had taken his own life.

Suicide was a terrible abomination. After night had fallen Ralph's body was taken to the crossroads at Corpse Cross, just outside the town. There it was buried without ceremony and a stake driven into the heart. This was the only certain way to prevent the unquiet spirit from rising and creating mayhem among the living.

But such terrible goings on did not need to prevent a happy occasion, the marriage of Clara Markey and James Rudhall, from going ahead. Just two days afterwards Clara was led down the aisle of St Mary's by her proud father, though there were some there that said he almost had to drag her.

Everything carried on normally until the clergyman turned to Clara and intoned, "Do you, Clara, take this man…?" Before he could finish Clara let out a frightful shriek that echoed through the rafters of the church and tickled the necks of all present. She gathered up her gown and would have run out of the church if not held by a group of her female relatives. For a while they tried to force her back to the chancel steps but, seeing the madness in her eyes, they helped her out and back to Alton Court, where she lay as if in a trance. Mr Markey did his best to smooth ruffled Rudhall feathers.

When he eventually returned home he went up to see his daughter. Her room was empty. Desperate servants went in search of her and eventually she was found at the Alton Road crossroads, prostrate over the newly dug grave, while a carter, whose trade was being held up, was trying gently to persuade her to move.

Of course the news was soon all over Ross and Clara's secret exposed to public gossip. Mr Markey kept her to her room, in the attempt to lessen the scandal but, at every opportunity, she would escape. They always knew where to find her, Corpse Cross. Inevitably she wore her father down and he let her make her journey every day without hindrance, knowing that, after nightfall, she would make her way back. So her life passed, caught up in grief and a deep madness that protects a mind from thought. She became a familiar sight to the people of Ross. When they heard that serious illness had come upon her and she was not expected to see out the week, many pitied her for the life she had led. Others thought it was a merciful release.

But it was not to be. Perhaps there is something that so much becomes part of your life that mere death cannot stop you from carrying it on. Just a few days after Clara's death was reported, several people, by no means the most disreputable of society, swore they had seen her taking her customary walk. Over the years it became an accepted part of Ross lore that, if you were in a particular part of the town when the light was falling, you too might see the figure of a young woman in old-fashioned clothes slowly pacing along the street that is still called Old Maid's Walk, as if unaware of her surroundings, as if drawn by a power stronger than death.

THE APOTHECARY'S
APPRENTICE

After some busy sightseeing, a tired female tourist sat down in High Town, the central piazza of Hereford, for a well-earned rest.

It was not to last long. An old man plonked himself down by her side so aggressively that the seat rocked back, frightening her for a moment that it would fall backwards. He let out a terrible sigh that seemed to indicate all too clearly that he had no idea of being quiet.

"Warm today."

"Yes, it is." She hoped it would be enough not to appear standoffish but not encourage conversation.

"You a visitor then?"

Although the word rather grated on her, she nodded as a way of limiting the conversation.

"You see that old black and white house over there? A few years back it moved."

"Really." Why do country people think they can fool people in this way? Some deep-seated inferiority complex no doubt.

"No, it's true enough. It got up on stilts and walked over there and then came back again." He laughed at his great wit.

"'Course, it didn't do it itself. It was property developers what did it. They wanted to build that store and the Council wouldn't let 'em tear down that old house so they put it on stilts, moved it out of the way until they'd built it and then stuck it back there. They were giants in those days right enough."

"Oh, I see."

"Sad thing was, all that moving about put paid to the

ghost." He looked over at her to see what reaction that had produced. She was looking at her watch.

"I better tell you the story," he said quickly.

We like to encourage the young but we do not like them becoming better at our trade than we are. It is ungrateful and disrespectful.

Gregory Price was an apothecary. He had a shop on the south side of High Town. It was a good place to have an apothecary's shop because town life, with all its anxieties and disappointments, puts many people in need of the services of an apothecary, while living in a town meant they had little access to herbs or the services of a hedge doctor.

So g̶   ̶ness that Gregory made the
momento̶   ̶ing on an apprentice. He had
lived alo̶   ̶ne and was not pleased with the
prospect̶   ̶er living soul under his roof, but
he was ̶   ̶life that meant working from light
in the ̶   ̶arkness at night, and sometimes
even d̶   ̶ght. When he was not dealing with
custor̶   ̶ he had to be preparing potions
and p̶   ̶is eyesight and his back becoming
troub̶   ̶becoming harder.
I̶   ̶ out on the water and mentioned it
to h̶   ̶ associates that he was looking for a
suit̶

sor̶   ̶ut also a little angry that no one should
co̶   ̶ his noble profession. Then, on a busy

Wednesday, a boy came into the shop accompanied by his mother. Unexpectedly it was the boy who did most of the talking while the mother stood nervously by the door. He claimed that he came from generations of healers but now wanted to learn the art of the apothecary. He believed that this joining together would do good for mankind.

Apothecary Price was not impressed. He had never liked country healers, who he saw as taking money from him unfairly. Working with one who had been trained in this uncivilised art did not fill him with pleasant bodings. However, this was the only one that had come forward. If he dismissed him then heaven knows when the next would come calling.

The boy, who went by the name of John Sevenoaks, was duly indentured and set to learning his trade. Given the boy's worrying pride in knowing things already, Gregory had been fearful that he would be stubborn and obstinate and difficult to teach but this was not the case. The boy was anxious to learn; in fact it sometimes gave Gregory a headache, so many questions the boy asked. It was very draining. Gregory was at least relieved that the boy did not have to be told a second time. What he was told he retained. In this way he had very quickly come to be an asset to the business. He seemed honest as well so that it was not too long before Gregory felt that he could leave his apprentice in charge of the shop when he went herb collecting or just strolling through Hereford in the manner of a burgess.

One warm summer's day he was doing just that. It had struck him that, with time on his hands, he could put himself forward as an Alderman of the City. He had always dismissed the idea before but now he saw that he could take on the importance that his place in the city deserved.

With this thought in mind he returned to the shop. He was just on the point of opening the door when he saw a long-time female customer of his already in the shop and shaking John's hand.

"Thank you so much young man," he heard her say. "You've cured me where that Old Price could do nothing for me."

The woman jumped as he entered and both she and the boy's faces were red, although John was still beaming at the compliment.

From thinking of plans for the future, Gregory Price's mind now began to think of altogether darker things. Was this all a ploy to supplant him? Had those rival herbalists out in the country heard of his skills and were now intent on replacing him with one of their own? He should have been more suspicious of this knave but now he had learned his lesson.

From then on Gregory began to watch the boy and his forebodings were rewarded. He made a point of absenting himself from the shop at regular intervals and noticed that more people came into the shop when John was serving than when he himself was present. He secretly eavesdropped on his apprentice and heard him doling out remedies that Gregory had not approved; this made all the more galling because those customers often came back into the shop to thank John on their efficacy, something that rarely happened to Gregory. Before long people were coming in and thanking John even when Gregory was present and seemed to think he would be pleased by this. Gregory feared the next phase of the operation to remove him was starting to take shape.

He was not going to let it happen. The advantage of being an apothecary is that you have all kinds of drugs and herbs readily to hand, not all of them of curative properties. The advantage of having an apprentice is that he is also readily to hand, sharing meals, drinking water from jugs that you can avoid.

In a few weeks John was complaining of a fever and stomach cramps. Gregory tried to minister to him but it did no good and John soon could not be roused from his bed. The symptoms exacerbated and, after two days of suffering, the boy was dead.

It is not the best publicity for an apothecary, for their apprentice to die of something that he cannot treat. There were certainly whispers around the town but no one was going to talk too openly about an important citizen and, in weighing scandal against the life of an apprentice, the mayor and corporation were certainly in favour of silence.

So Gregory Price returned to the life of a solitary. He was not an evil man. He regretted what he had done, but business is business. He expected the child's mother to come and rant at him but no one came, though he lived in fear of it for several weeks, but then it dawned on him that he had got away with it.

Late one night he became annoyed with his apprentice for making such a noise in his room. He was about to get out and tell the boy to stop when he remembered there was no one alive in that room next to his. He lay awake listening to those knockings and footsteps. Occasionally they sounded as if they were coming closer, just the other side of the wall, then, in an instant, they seemed to be in a far part of the house. There was no sleep for Gregory. The following day his customers noted his distraction and how he would jump when anyone entered the shop.

Every night it became the same. Once Gregory found the courage to go into that room; as he expected it was completely empty. He was both relieved and very scared, for the sounds continued around him as he stood there in the empty bedroom that still had the boy's bed in it. In the candlelight, Gregory started seeing shapes and movement. He dropped the candle and ran out of the room.

He could get no sleep. An apothecary has means of dealing with that problem, but what had worked in the past made no difference now. So he started taking stronger mixtures. Too strong. One morning he was found dead in his bed, a look of abject terror on his face.

In the course of time new people moved into the shop but they too heard the noises. When they told of it people put two and two together and suspicions grew about Gregory's guilt.

For many years it was the same. But, after the house was moved and then brought back again, the noises seem to have ceased.

Then the old man was up and off across High Town without another word. For a moment the woman stayed looking at the old black and white house. When she turned and searched for the old man she had lost him in the crowd.

THE LEGEND OF
GOODRICH CASTLE

Cavalier or Roundhead? We all have an opinion, whether we are supporters of Parliament or the King, without fully understanding the contemporary arguments. But that was true of the people of the time. Whom you supported depended very much on where you lived, what the people around you said and what your landlord told you to do. Most people just wanted to keep out of it.

Herefordshire was mostly Royalist. Hereford, after withstanding a siege by an army of Scots under the Earl of Leven, fell by a trick by the new Parliamentary commander, Colonel John Birch, a Bristol man. Originally nothing more than a packhorse driver, he had fought off a gang of Cavaliers and earned a commission from Oliver Cromwell himself. He was known to be a cold man, more interested in what was in it for Colonel Birch than to be liked. But he was cunning. Disguising some toughs from the Forest of Dean as ordinary workmen, they approached Bysters Gate on a cold dawn and engaged the guards in conversation, then killed them with their spades and pickaxes, enabling the attacking force, which had been hidden in the ruins of St Guthlac's priory, to capture the town before the Royalists knew what was happening.

A small force of die-hard Royalists, under the command of Sir Harry Lingen, escaped from the mayhem and rode to Goodrich Castle and set about fortifying what was already a bit of a ruin. From there they would ride out and harry any Roundheads they could find, much to the displeasure of Col Birch. No one likes it to be thought that they cannot keep control of a situation.

The winter of 1645 to '46 was a harsh one. It is a sad fact that, in all wars, more people die of hunger and disease than get killed in the actual fighting. That winter there was many a Herefordshire mother who called down curses on both sides as her children starved in front of her.

One morning, through a flurry of snow, the guard at Goodrich spotted two riders approaching. After assurances of their peaceful intentions they were let into the castle. Sir Harry recognised one of them, Charles Clifford, of a good Royalist family. The other was introduced to him as Alice Birch, niece of the Colonel who had put a price on Sir Harry's head.

Inside the tower of the castle, near a pitiful fire that did little to counteract the bitter chill in the room, Clifford told their story. He had gone to see Col Birch to negotiate a safe passage for some of his family. Birch had kept him waiting and, as he kicked his heels, he fell into conversation with a young woman. The conversation became so enjoyable to both the young man and the young woman that they wished to repeat it. Finding out the other person's identity only gave excitement to the secret meetings rather than put an end to them.

In the end, knowing that neither family would take well to the news of their love for each other, they decided that the only way to remain together was to elope. Clifford suggested the only place in Herefordshire that might welcome them and Alice had agreed.

Sir Harry listened quietly. When Charles had finished

he sighed and said, "Of course you can find shelter here if you ask for it. But I must warn you that this will be no easy thing. Our lives hang by a thread and yours will too if you remain."

Alice stepped forward and spoke for the first time. "Thank you for your kindness and your frankness. In return let me tell you that my uncle is planning an attack on you."

"I expected no less."

"It will come next Saturday."

Sure enough, that Saturday morning, a large Roundhead force left Hereford heading south towards Goodrich. It was evening by the time it arrived. Though snow remained on the fields the army had soon churned the road to icy mud. There had been no time to send for heavy cannon but Col Birch hoped to take the garrison by surprise and frighten them into surrender. He was annoyed when, on his first glimpse of the castle, he saw the gates closed and men with muskets already on the ramparts.

Under a flag of truce he went forward to advise the garrison of their position but was met by only by laughter and insults. Then a cold fear entered his heart. Where were Lingen and the other notables? These were only a few gutter sweepings. He was a skilled soldier and he was fearful of what this might mean.

Leaving his foot soldiers to burn the stables and other buildings outside the walls and return as best they could, he hurried back to Hereford with his men of horse. It was a treacherous undertaking, they only had the light from the snowy fields to guide them.

When they reached Hereford, Birch's worst fears were confirmed. Lingen had attacked and had quickly dispatched the small garrison that had been left there but, being a skilled soldier himself, knew that he did not have enough men to hold the city and had escaped over the frozen River Wye back to Goodrich.

Now John Birch was angry. He ordered the iron founders of the city to build the greatest siege cannon that had even been built in England. "Roaring Meg" her gunners called her. Birch watched her test firings on the water meadows east of the city and a smile came to his face for the first time in weeks.

He and his army returned to Goodrich and he took Roaring Meg with him. Slowly she bit away at the medieval walls and the nerves of the garrison.

Imagine what it was like for Alice, the only woman in the castle. No privacy, little food and water and always the cries of the wounded; always waiting for the next crump from Roaring Meg and then waiting for the shock against the wall.

Charles Clifford went to Sir Harry and told him that he had to get Alice away.

"I don't disagree with you. The problem will be how to manage it."

The frost turned to thaw, but with it came heavy rain. The mud made everyone's life a misery, Roundhead or Cavalier. Sir Harry called Charles. "If you want to go this is your time. The rain is better than fog because it will keep the Puritans' heads down. You might try and swim a horse across the river but it will not be an easy task."

Charles went to see Alice and they agreed that it was their best hope. Her uncle would find no mercy for Charles and little for his niece if they surrendered to him. Charles saddled his horse and Alice in her riding cloak climbed up behind him.

As soon as the horse came out from the shelter of the walls the cold rain beat on its flanks like sleet. It shied but Charles drove it forward to the riverbank. The river was in flood and running fast. The horse again stopped and its white, terrified eyes reflected the dark torrent in front of it, but still Charles drove it on. Uneasily it stepped into the water. It struggled in the strong current. It fought for its life and it fought hard, but the strength of the river was too much for it. For a moment there were screams, cries and the neighing of a frightened horse; then silence.

Sir Harry held out until the spring but then the food, water and ammunition ran out and he was forced to come to terms with Col Birch. They were allowed to march out with honour, flags flying and still with their arms and with their little band playing the tune, "Sir Harry Lingen's Fancy."

Goodrich Castle is a quiet place now. Its peace and quiet only occasionally interrupted by the cries of tourists and battle re-enactors. But people who go there at night, especially if it is a wet night and the river is in flood, have heard the sound of the terrified neighs of a horse fighting for its life and the cries of lovers being torn apart by the flood.

ROGER DE CLIFFORD

Roger de Clifford was not an evil man. However, he was an important and rich nobleman; inevitably there were things that he did that made him wake up sweating in the dark hours of the night. There were people that needed killing, not always in fair fight, there were deals to be made rarely equitable to the other party and he had fought against his king, Edward II, not because the man was a poor king but because Roger saw a chance to get even richer and more powerful.

As he felt his body getting weaker these things played on his mind more and more. Would his soul be damned for eternity because he had done what felt like the right thing? His mother, in the last years of her life, had retreated to the nunnery at Aconbury, south of Hereford. He had seen that it had given her a great deal of consolation and she had been buried in the chapel. He entered into negotiations with the nuns so that he also would be interred there. In return for a substantial amount of money the nuns would say a mass for his soul every day. Surely that would waft him safely to heaven?

As he had feared it was not long before Sir Roger took to his deathbed and, after not too long a struggle, departed this life. His body was taken to Aconbury and deposited in a fine stone tomb. The establishment greatly enriched by Sir Roger's beneficence, the nuns sang joyfully for the salvation of his soul. They also used the money to set up a noted centre of learning for young women, so many had cause to thank the memory of Sir Roger.

So it continued for two hundred years. How far Sir Roger had risen up the ranks of Purgatory it is impossible to say but clearly not far enough, from what happened next.

By the early sixteenth century a double force was working against the continued existence of places of religious life such as Aconbury. Reformers wanted to sweep away these trappings of idolatry, while conservative forces, who might be expected to protect the status quo, thought of the vast wealth that would come their way. In 1536 an Act of Parliament dissolved the smaller monasteries and nunneries, Aconbury among them. The nuns received a pension and were sent out into the world, the Masses stopped. The land was sold off and most of the stone torn down for building material. What remained became the small church of a poor parish.

Some of the oldsters muttered that no good would come of it and they were right. The verger, generally considered a steady man, gave up his post and moved to the town, saying that he could cope with moaning parishioners but he was not going to put up with ghosts. The newly-appointed incumbent, Miles Taylor, a man of zeal who was determined to drag his flock into the modern era, whether they wanted to come or not, a man who believed in the certainties of Providence, not the superstitious mumblings of the past, was disconcerted, one Sunday morning, to see the figure of a medieval knight striding towards him down the bare chancel. Fortunately there was a back door but he would never be alone in his own church from that point, even in the daylight. He was considered outrageous for taking his dog into the church, but the real reason was he hoped the dog would sense the spirit first and enable him to make a run for it.

Just as there are nice drunks and nasty ones, there are nice and nasty ghosts and Sir Roger clearly fell into the latter category. He was angry and determined to let everyone know. He developed an unpleasant habit of manifesting himself near his tomb and lunging at anyone who had the misfortune to be passing. The parishioners begged Miles Taylor to perform an exorcism but he would have none of it. He would have nothing to do with such mummery, even though he had as good cause as any to know the need. So it went on throughout the long years that Mr Taylor remained in his place, much as he made every effort to find a better one. Even when he eventually succeeded the new vicar was of a like mind and refused to countenance papist nonsense in the shape of exorcism, though he was the victim of more than one appearance by Sir Roger. As if gaining strength by this lack of action or perhaps just getting ever more angry, the ghost was now appearing not only within the confines of the church. People reported seeing the figure lurking in the churchyard. Going to church or even merely walking by it became an act of trepidation.

But fashions, even in the matter of ghosts, change. Archbishop Laud determined that Puritanism was no way to heaven and that a bit more ceremony would be no bad thing. Gerald Staite, the man who now was vicar of Aconbury, quite liked showing off, as some of his more hard-line parishioners saw it, and decided that here was a good opportunity to get rid of the ghost.

He visited his fellow clergy of the Deanery to discuss what needed to be done. No one was too sure, it was beyond living memory since anything like this had been carried out. Old books were consulted. Everybody agreed that bell, bibles and candles were involved and the more vicars the better, for added piety. But not one of the other clergymen wanted to get mixed up in it. So poor Rev Gerald Staite found himself alone at midnight in his empty church.

He lit the special beeswax candle and then reluctantly blew out his lantern, plunging the church into almost darkness, only that small light surrounding his body and a lot of shadow beyond. He knelt on the cold, hard stone floor beside Sir Roger's tomb, clasped his Bible tightly and rang the handbell. It had sounded deeply sonorous in the vicarage but, in the empty church, it tinkled rather weakly.

Mr Staite prayed fervently, more than he had ever done so in his life, and he was noted in the parish for his zeal. He prayed until the sweat poured down his back, until he felt another presence behind him. Barely able to turn he saw, out of the corner of his eye, a grey shape and he felt a breath on the nape of his neck that made him shiver. The candle guttered and he knew that, if it were to be extinguished, the ghost would win.

He re-doubled his prayers, his Bible greasy with his own sweat, his eyes blinded with salt. The dead breath blew and the candle flame flashed horizontal, the seats and walls of the church dancing madly in the approaching darkness. But still he prayed and he felt the ghost weakening. It might have been an hour, it might have been forever, that fight until Mr Staite, at last, knew he was winning and gaining power over the ghost. Still, he did not slacken but pressed on until the thing behind him was no more than a small grey mist just above the floor. Then he reached for the old cider bottle that he had brought for the purpose and scooped the mist into it and quickly put the stopper on. Leaving it on the church floor he dragged his feet out of the building, slumped on a gravestone and waited for the dawn. Never had his heart rejoiced so much to see the first fingers of light. As the sky lightened above him he breathed in its beauty and resolved that he would greet every dawn from now on and give thanks for his deliverance.

When it was fully light he dared return to the site of the battle. The church was as cold as a tomb but the bottle lay quiet where he had left it. He reached for a small pick that he had brought with him and started to work away at the mortar around a stone in the wall. There was something almost sacrilegious in the deed but, emboldened by his night's work, he scraped away until the stone was free. He had thought of asking the local stonemason to help him but had resolved that this was a job in which he could involve no one else. When the stone was free he took the bottle and carefully placed it in a recess behind the stone, lifted the stone and put it back. Now the spirit was confined and buried neither in the church nor without and would lose all power. He went home, longing for his bed. He would let the mason re-mortar the stone later in the day. Then the stones could be quiet for eternity.

Mr Staite was a local hero. His parishioners bragged

him up to strangers and considered themselves lucky to have such a good shepherd. But some worry remained. All authorities said that a silver box should be used to imprison the spirit but where could a poor clergyman find such a thing? He comforted himself that cider bottles were strong. It would hold.

Of course he knew nothing of the expansion and contraction of materials with temperature change. Two hundred years of frost and sun took their toll and in 1863 the bottle cracked and Sir Roger was released, his temperament not improved by the indignity meted out to him. Now he did not so much haunt as stalk. Those who now saw him reported that he was not so much lunging but reaching out for them as if seeking to drag them down to the hell that he came from. Naturally, most people fled before he got even close. But young Jim Maddocks, for a bet, spent one warm summer night sitting on a gravestone daring the ghost to come to him. He lost the bet, returning in the small hours, white-faced, with the story that the ghost had crept up on him and touched him on his right shoulder before he had ran for it. People laughed and took it for a jest but Jimmy Maddocks was dead within two months and the regular congregation at St John's plummeted. Even walking along the road by it was looked on as an act of the highest bravery or stupidity, depending on whom you talked to. The graves became unkempt because no one wanted to spend time caring for them.

When the diocese was looking for churches to be declared redundant perhaps it was no surprise that

Aconbury was top of the list. So this sad little church remains, kept mostly locked and the small churchyard having a mournful air. Those with a romantic disposition, or a hankering after danger, are welcome to visit it.

THE CWN ANNWN

In the old days, when the occasional wolf still roamed the Welsh hills and might come over and prey on Herefordshire flocks, there lived an old widow woman and her three sons.

They rented a small farm near the village of Eardisley that could barely support three people, let alone four, so it was not surprising that there were quite a few tensions in the household.

The sons were called Tom, Dick and Posthumous. The mother had wanted to call the last son Harry, but the local clergyman, who was a learned man, said that this name was the correct one, since the baby had been born after the death of his father.

There was a ten-year age gap between the two elder brothers and the younger, so that, when Tom and Dick were of an age that they were having to work hard on the farm, Posthumous was still sticking close to his mother's apron strings. As often happens the young one, the one that a mother knows will be the last born, held a special place in her heart. You could not blame the older brothers being somewhat resentful about all of this.

The year that Posthumous turned twelve was a particularly cold winter. There was no activity on the farm and very little food. The only things to do were to hope that what food there was would last until the first crops in the summer and to go out and collect firewood.

With each frozen day that passed those two activities became harder. The three brothers had to travel further to find wood and carry it back over longer distances knowing that, even so, they were going back to a cold house and the approach of misery.

It was the time of the full moon and, somehow, that made the nights feel even colder. Staring down from the star-lit sky, the bright moon seemed to cast a chill onto the countryside and the warmth of the sun seemed a distant memory.

The brothers' efforts to gather firewood had been poor over the last few days so that, on this, what was going to be the coldest night of the year, they could see that they did not have enough to keep the fire going through the night. The brothers knew that, while it would be uncomfortable for them, for their poor old mother it might be her last night on earth if the cold got into her bones.

"We must go out and get more," said Tom.

"But it's dark and we will have to travel a long way," said Posthumous.

"If you're afraid, you don't have to come," said Dick.

Of course Posthumous was afraid, but he still insisted on coming. When their old mother saw them putting on their rabbit-fur jerkins she did not try to stop Tom or Dick but she did beg them not to take Posthumous. Although it did not have any effect it was another little sliver of resentment that went into their hearts to add to all the others.

They set off into the frosty moonlight, banging their hands on their shoulders to try to keep off the shivers, their breaths steaming in the chill.

It seemed to them that they must have trudged miles

before they came to Lord Baskerville's Wood. As they walked along its boundaries they could hear the boughs of the great trees crashing together in the wind.

"There's plenty of wood in there. Why don't we take some of that?" asked Posthumous.

The two other brothers laughed.

"That's Lord Baskerville's land. Only his tenants can take wood from it," said Tom. "If any of his men catch you taking any wood they'll hang you from the tree you got it from."

"Either that," said Dick, "Or the Cwn Annwn will get you."

"What's that?"

"They are the hounds of hell; spirits in the shape of dogs that hunt in the air. They are blacker than the night. They are sent by the devil himself to hunt out wicked souls and to drag them down into hell."

They stood still, listening to the tormented branches smacking against each other in the wood.

"Our mother needs the wood. There it is, easily taken. I'm going into the Wood."

"Please yourself. You can't say we didn't warn you," said Tom and he walked off.

"We'll tell mother that when you don't come home," laughed Dick as he followed.

Posthumous stood still for a moment, listening to the chuckles of his brothers getting fainter and fainter. When it was silent he turned and faced the Wood. With a deep breath he walked under the trees.

With the heaving branches overhead, the storm

seemed worse in here. The enormity of what he was doing hit him like the wind. This was stealing, and worse, stealing from a lord. He could easily think that the devil would loose his hounds on him.

He started collecting some of the wood that had been blown down by the wind. He had barely started when he heard a noise that made him stop. The howl of a hound. Then it was answered by another, closer howl. Posthumous stood still, his legs frozen with terror.

The howls were getting close, the noise of a whole pack and Posthumous felt they were coming straight for him. He started to run, further into the forest, but that did not stop the sounds from getting ever closer. Soon he could hear the paws crashing through the leaves.

He came out into a clearing, which was the last thing he wanted to do, feeling that the dogs were right behind him. He had run into the centre when he tripped on a concealed root and fell flat on his face. Although winded he span around onto his back to see what was coming.

Out of the darkness of the trees came a huge shape, much larger than any dog he had seen. As it moved further into the clearing he saw it had pale, shaggy fur and a long snout – a wolf. Behind it came another and then another. It gave him no pleasure to see these were not the hounds of hell. From their deliberate way they came out of the clearing they might as well have been.

The largest of the wolves, the one he had first seen, came closer to him and then sat down not three yards away. The other wolves followed until they had made a circle all around him. The whole world had fallen silent.

Posthumous felt strangely calm. There was nothing he could do now.

Then the wolf leader raised its head and started to sing. It started to sing the special wolf song to the moon. One by one the other wolves joined in. They sang of a time when forest covered the land and hunting was easy. A time before man had grown so plentiful that he had crowded out all other life. A good time that had gone and would never come again. Posthumous felt the sadness of it in the pit of his stomach and cold tears rolled down his face. As quickly as it had started the wolf leader fell silent and the others also ended their song. The big wolf sat and looked at Posthumous and the boy felt the large black eyes burning into him. Then the wolf got up and brushed by him. He felt the touch of its fur and smelled the deep smell of wild nature. The other wolves also rose and they trotted off together into the blackness of the trees on the other side of the clearing. After a while he heard their call deep within the trees and then he felt the cold bite into him again and he forced himself to get up.

He walked back through the trees, collecting firewood as he went so that, by the time he came out at the edge of the wood, he had a burden almost too heavy to carry. Yet that did not worry him now. He felt as if nothing could touch him. He walked the long distance home yet it only seemed a few minutes before he was pushing open the heavy wooden door. His mother and brothers were huddled over what remained of the fire. They looked shocked to see him. His brothers rose and rushed forward to embrace him.

"We thought you were dead," said Tom.

"We heard the wolves," said Dick.

"No, I'm fine," said Posthumous. "Let's get this wood on the fire before we all die of the cold."

And so they did, and for many nights later, so that they made it through that winter. Posthumous never told anyone of what happened to him in the wood. People from that part rarely talk about their dealings with the supernatural. But after that time he was changed. People said he had a feeling for nature. They brought sick animals to him to be cured and asked his advice about planting their crops so that he was considered a great man in the neighbourhood. For that night he had been given a special gift, to see the Earth as it was meant to be.

LORD EDVIN AND
LORD RALPH

The Bastard had swept most of the old Saxon nobility away. New men, searching for land, riches and power, roamed the land.

Two such men were Lord Ralph and Lord Edvin. They were foster brothers. It was the fashion for sons of gentlemen to spend their childhoods in the household of greater lords, there to learn the ways of the world and the skills of arms. Both boys had been fostered by a Marcher Lord on the Welsh borders. There they had learned good sword skills and the belief that a sword will give them what they wanted. Do it to somebody else before they do it to you. Bitterness had crept into their souls.

But they were successful. Having started out quite poor, they had, between them, amassed a good amount of wealth. This had attracted others of their kind so that they could call on a fearsome private army. It meant that there were not many in the county of Herefordshire who could take them on in a fight. People were respectful to them and they developed the reputation of quick tempers to make people even more respectful.

For all their riches, the one thing they could never gain was satisfaction. There were always new extortions that could be made, there were always even uglier men at their own backs that needed paying. If you had asked them when they were young how much wealth they wanted and they had given you a figure, well, now they had long exceeded that amount but still they could not stop. It struck them that they had the talent to become some of the greatest lords in the country.

Like all such nobles, the manors they held were spread around Herefordshire, but most of them fell in the northeast part of the county. That was the area they considered their power base. So it was hurtful to them that they were not the most powerful lords there. That distinction went to Radulfus de Zedefen, Lord of Yedefen. At the mention of his name, both Edvin and Ralph would become foul-tempered and vicious.

Radulfus had a daughter, Maud, his only child. She was by popular assent the most beautiful young woman in Herefordshire, and also one with the largest dowry. She was a target too tempting to ignore. In the evenings, as they drank with their cronies, Edvin and Ralph vied with each other in the things they would do to her when she was in their power. Yet they knew that time was not yet come. Radulfus could still command greater forces then they had available. But they bided their time because they knew that would change. Radulfus was an old man.

Of course Radulfus could see what was happening and, if he had been a more warlike man, he would have attacked them first before they could come against him. He had searched his conscience and decided that it was his Christian duty to turn away from such a thing. While he had fought in many battles and skirmishes as a young man and had achieved a reputation for his skill in the tournament, he had always put his faith in the Church. Now the years had bitten away at him and he felt ever closer to Judgement he could not bring himself to be the aggressor, even though he knew it was probably the most sensible thing to do.

The power of Ralph and Edvin grew ever greater and Radulfus felt that the time was coming close when they would be strong enough to come against him. Now it was too late he regretted not having taken action before and reproached himself for such laxity that could only bring horror on his child.

His daughter Maud saw that worry. Before he had been pleased to take her with him when he travelled and delighted in showing her the wonder of God's creation, now he became fretful if she wanted to leave the castle and she would often find him sitting alone and troubled in the evening.

Her mother had been a Welsh princess from one of the many royal bloodlines of the many petty kingdoms. Although she was now dead she had taught her daughter many of the strange arts that they practise over the border. While her father would never have told her of the fears that were causing him worry, from listening to the talk of people that ladies of pure Norman blood would never have listened to she saw into her father's anxiety. If she had been of pure Norman blood and heard the gossip about what the two foster brothers had planned for her she might have sighed and thought, well, at least the two of them have money. A girl could do worse. They would probably fight each other for her hand; that would have its attractions. But she had different blood flowing through her veins. She had already made her choice. Her eye had already fallen on Thomas, her father's squire, a man comely and kind. She made plans. She knew that her father was sad that his illustrious name would die out. Thomas would change his name to de Zedefen, she would marry Thomas and so name and bloodline would stay in Herefordshire. She was not going to let a couple of louts spoil those plans.

One afternoon she went down to the river near her castle, actually no more than a stream, a tributary of the River Frome. She walked along the bank until she saw what she wanted, a couple of swans feeding on the river. She sat down on the bank quietly, so as not to disturb them and she watched the pen swan intently. So intently that she could feel the cold water on her breast, the pull of the current on her feet; through her eyes she could see the dappled greenery of the trees contrasting with the blue dress of the woman watching her from the bank.

That afternoon Ralph and Edvin were out hunting. If there was no one to bully it was the occupation they enjoyed the best. They mounted their fine horses, grabbed their sharp boar spears and shouted at the hunting dogs. They rode off from their manor of Buckenhall in the direction of the land of Radulfus de Zedefen. If they did not find a boar perhaps their dogs would bring down some of his sheep and who knows what trouble that could lead to.

They were just riding over a bridge above a stream of a tributary of the River Frome when they both looked to their left and saw a fine swan swimming down the river towards them.

"That swan would make a fine feast," said Ralph.

"It would indeed," said Edvin. "You ride over to the far bank and I'll go to the near and we'll spear it as it comes from under the bridge."

So they both dismounted and took their places opposite each other on the two river banks, each holding their spears aloft in delightful anticipation of the swan swimming out under the bridge.

Perhaps they were not as quiet as they thought they had been because, when the swan came from under the bridge it was flying, not swimming. Neither wanted to miss their prey so both threw their spears at the flying bird. The spear of Lord Ralph flew over the swan and buried itself in the chest of Lord Edvin. The spear of Lord Edvin flew under the swan and buried itself in the chest of Lord Ralph. Both men fell backwards, dead, onto the river bank.

The swan flew up and then circled the bridge, its wings thrumming in triumph and then flew back the way it had come.

Maud lay on the river bank. She was soaking wet and her arms and legs hurt, but there was a smile on her face. After thanking the swan, who looked a little bemused, she got up and made her way back to her father's castle.

Now, if her plans to marry Thomas were successful, I cannot say. But I do know that if you go to Edvin Ralph church there are some wonderful stone effigies of knights and their ladies. On one of them is this inscription:

"Here lies the Lady Maud. She was the wife of Sir Thomas de Edifen. To whomsoever shall say a

Pater and an Ave for the soul of Maud de Edifen, the Lord Bishop of Worcester will allow thirty days of pardon, and the Lord Bishop of Hereford sixty days of pardon."

If you go to that church and you say those prayers… well, you could do a lot worse.